A GARDEN FAIR

A GARDEN FAIR

Helen McCabe

CHIVERS

British Library Cataloguing in Publication Data available

This Large Print edition published by BBC Audiobooks Ltd, Bath, 2008.
Published by arrangement with the Author.

U.K. Hardcover ISBN 978 1 405 64454 9
U.K. Softcover ISBN 978 1 405 64455 6

Printed and bound in Great Britain by
Antony Rowe Ltd., Chippenham, Wiltshire

CHAPTER ONE

Cathy broke the tiny, heart-shaped pudding in two with her fork. It was Marie's speciality, coeurs a la crème, made of ricotta cheese, cream, fresh fruit and raspberry sauce. She put a piece of the scrumptious dessert into her mouth; it tasted as delicious as it looked. But nothing can mend my broken heart, she thought whimsically, then told herself that was nonsense, as she'd never really been in love with Paul. She only thought she had. Which was what hurt the most after he dumped her. How could she have been so silly to be taken in by him?

She sighed, then remembered where she was. She should be happy. She was on holiday for the whole summer in Chinon, an ancient town, set on the banks of a sleepy tributary of the River Loire.

Marie Laine was her mother's oldest friend and her house was a lovely, old place near to the castle, which dominated the town. Chinon Castle had been built so high, that it was murder on your legs, if you dared to climb up the rock. The castle was closely associated with Joan of Arc and when she was very young, Cathy loved her mother to tell her the story of how the girl saint, who saved France from the English had found the Dauphin straightaway,

1

when the heir to the French throne, staying at her court in Chinon, dressed himself in ordinary clothes and hid from her purposely amongst the crowd of his courtiers.

Although Cathy hadn't been a frequent visitor to her mother's old village, because her parents were constantly travelling and she was at boarding school, when she did visit Marie, she always felt she was coming to her second home. But it didn't stop her sighing about what had happened between her and Paul . . .

Cathy shook herself. She really had to make an effort and, lifting her head, looked brightly across at Marie's other guests. But she still wasn't taking in the lively conversation. She felt like an outsider and particularly guilty, knowing Marie had gone to such a lot of trouble to cheer her up.

'You seem sad, mam'selle.' The man opposite was smiling at her. Marie had introduced him earlier as Bernard de Benoit. The name rang a bell, but she couldn't quite place him. He was good-looking in a middle-aged way, but Cathy decided she didn't like his eyes, that didn't smile when he did. Earlier, he had been monopolising the conversation, telling everyone that he was going off to the United States on business for a whole month, the following day. He was evidently loaded.

His English was good too; much better than her French, at present. Cathy was bi-lingual, but being away at college and not practising the language, except when she went home, had made her a little rusty.

'I'm not sad,' she answered defensively.

'Cathy has been working very hard,' interposed Marie. Cathy warmed to her. Her mother's childhood friend was so sophisticated and elegant. She always said the right thing.

'I've just finished my college exams,' she explained. It was a good enough reason.

'Ah . . .' they chorused and continued to pick at their sweets as the French always did. In a very leisurely way, accompanied by excellent wine.

'Such hard work has taken the life out of her,' added Bernard facetiously.

'Cathy speaks very good French, don't you, dear,' prompted Marie, her eyes twinkling. 'In fact, you knew her mother, Bernard.' His eyebrows rose. 'Rosalie . . .'

'Rosalie . . .' He was thinking. 'Rosalie . . . not Rosalie Chene?'

'Rosalie Murdoch,' corrected Marie. 'My best friend went off and actually married an English civil servant but, happily, her daughter is as French as French can be.'

'In some ways,' replied Cathy guardedly. Bernard laughed.

'And what are those?'

'Food, wine and . . .' Suddenly, she didn't know what else.

'Love?' he asked. Marie saw Cathy's eyes flash. She was so much like her mother in

3

every way; not only had she the golden skin and tawny eyes, that characterised the girls of the region, but also the intelligence and wit.

'I don't think we should say anything else on that subject,' added Marie firmly.

'Thank you,' replied Cathy. She didn't want strangers knowing her business. And certainly not Monsieur Benoit. He was slimy!

'What are you studying?' asked the mayor. Marie knew everyone!

'Horticulture,' replied Cathy. 'Garden design, but eighteenth century, in particular.' A murmur of approval rippled round the table. The French loved their gardens—and their history.

'How interesting,' said Bernard, leaning back, sipping his red wine. 'I have a very large garden.'

'Bernard! It's an estate,' corrected the mayor's wife, laughing.

'Seventy-five hectares, in total,' he announced. Cathy was calculating. That was, at least, 185 acres!

'Good heavens,' she said.

'And it takes up so much time, he hasn't time to attend to pressing local matters,' added Marie pointedly. Cathy didn't think anything of the remark at the time, but she remembered it afterwards.

'Do you have many gardeners?' asked Cathy.

'Quite a few, but I can always use more. In

4

fact, I have a large, wayward plot, that needs a fresh outlook.'

'Cathy doesn't want to talk shop, Bernard. She's here for a holiday,' protested Marie.

'But I do!' cried Cathy.

'Well, why don't you come over and take a look?' he persisted.

'I thought you were going to New York,' said Marie.

'Unfortunately. But that doesn't matter. I would be really pleased if Mam'selle Cathy called and saw my agent, Dupont. The garden, I mean, is a special plot near the tributary of the lake . . .'

No-one could stop him after that. He was in full flow. When he'd finished, he said, 'I would so like to see that garden restored to its former glory. All the historic maps are in my library. This is a pet project of mine and I would be very glad of a fresh, young opinion.'

'But I'm not qualified yet,' replied Cathy. Her head was whirling. Here was a man ready to let her loose on his garden! 'I wouldn't want any payment either,' she added sincerely. 'I'd be glad to help.'

'A girl after my own heart,' said Bernard suavely. 'Done!' He shook hands with her across the table. The mayor coughed.

Then Cathy noticed Bernard's eyes were glittering unpleasantly. She had been carried away with the idea. What was really behind this offer?

5

'If you would like to draw up some plans as to how you see the finished garden, I will consider them and—if I like them, I shall put them into action. In the meantime, you could start clearing the patch. In any case, I would be glad to pay you for that.'

'Thank you,' she said. In spite of her instincts, she realised that the man was offering what would be her first commission! Cathy imagined it heading her CV already . . . She looked over at Marie and to her astonishment, Marie's lips were drawn in a tight, thin line. Cathy could see that, for some strange reason, her mother's friend certainly did not approve.

'You should be out enjoying yourself in this vacation, rather than working,' said Marie as she stacked the dishwasher.

'But this is how I enjoy myself,' protested Cathy. 'Why don't you approve, Marie? Perhaps Monsieur Benoit was just being kind.'

'I doubt it,' Marie said. Cathy regarded her with astonishment. She sounded as if she really disliked Bernard. 'He says things he doesn't mean a lot of the time.'

'Oh, well, you've warned me,' replied Cathy lightly, although she felt just the opposite. 'Anyway, I'm going to go up there and see his agent. Where does the man hang out?'

'In the chateau's office. Dupont's quite nice, if a little lazy.'

'I'm glad someone's nice. You don't like

Bernard, do you, Marie?' Cathy usually spoke her mind.

'There, that's done.' Marie straightened up from the dishwasher. Cathy was puzzled. Was Marie going to ignore the question totally? But she hadn't expected the answer, when it came.

'I've known Bernard for a very long time. You have too, dear.'

'What do you mean?'

'I suppose you don't remember going up the chateau, do you?' Marie smiled inwardly as she thought of those good days. No-one could bring them back. Cameos in her memory. Riding in the old Renault 5. Rosalie laughing, throwing back her curls, which hung around her face like a Renaissance angel's. Cathy had hair just like her mother's but, that night, its gold was smoothed up and away from her face, although a few curls were already escaping.

'No, I don't think so. I was only a baby, wasn't I?' Cathy was at a loss.

'Maman and I used to take you up there in the little old car. You were in the carrycot. You liked gardens even then. Such wonderful summers. But that was when Bernard was universally liked.'

'What did he do that was so bad?' Cathy had been torturing her memory, trying to dredge up anything her mother had said about him.

'I can't tell you,' replied Marie firmly. 'And

7

what's more, it's not my place. You must form your own opinion. And I suspect you'll find out for yourself, if you're determined not to take my advice.'

'He'll be in the States anyway.' Cathy felt a little uncomfortable.

'So he said. He intends to, but one can never tell with Bernard.'

'So why did you invite him to dinner?' Cathy believed in being forthright.

'Difficult to say. I suppose . . . I hoped . . . that one day he might change.'

'Do people ever?' asked Cathy.

'You're very cynical,' smiled Marie. 'Sometimes they do. But rarely.'

'Somehow, I don't think there's much hope for Bernard,' replied Cathy. They looked at each other and laughed . . .

CHAPTER TWO

The next day Benoit's land agent, Dupont, took her over to see the garden. The chateau was impressive, but the allocated patch was all that Benoit had indicated—an overgrown and neglected piece of land.

'This is it,' indicated Dupont. She could read the look on his face. He thought she was crazy! Although Marie had said he was a nice man, Cathy wasn't sure. He evidently didn't approve of a complete stranger coming to take over a piece of the land for which he was responsible.

'It's marvellous,' said Cathy, opening the door of the mud-spattered Land Rover. She had been surprised when he jumped in the vehicle, thinking that they would be walking to the plot. It wasn't that far from the chateau, but, looking at Dupont, she concluded he preferred driving to exercise. Marie had been right, he probably was lazy. It showed in his weight.

'You think so?' was the dour reply. The large man leaned against the door, with a wry expression on his face.

'Yes, I do.'

'I'm glad to hear you think it's exciting, mam'selle, but—what exactly do you intend to do?'

'I mean to clear it,' replied Cathy, thrusting her hands into the pockets of her jeans. 'And plant it—in time.'

'Not on your own?' He looked horrified.

'Well . . .' She grimaced. ' . . . I thought that Monsieur Benoit meant to offer me a little help, as soon as he's approved the plans, of course.'

'What kind of help?' Dupont was a man of few words.

'I assume I'd have the loan of a tractor and a rotovator.' She knew she was being cheeky but she'd actually seen both in one of the outbuildings. In fact, there were two of the latter. 'I can drive machines.'

He lifted one eyebrow in disbelief. 'My gardeners have a full schedule,' he replied unhelpfully, 'but, seeing that you're here on the boss's orders, I expect it would be all right. I mean . . . I could lend you one of the men to get started.'

'That would be delightful,' said Cathy. She hadn't been looking forward to using either machine. It was true she knew how to but it would have been a bit sticky to actually carry out all the rough jobs on her own. Bernard had plenty of gardeners. It showed in the way the chateau was kept. Pristine, which made it all the more peculiar why he kept one plot of land in such an awful state.

'If you tell me what you want, I'll try to sort it out for you but . . .' he hesitated, ' . . . but I have to check it out with the boss first. He'll be ringing me after he lands.'

He doesn't believe I have permission, thought Cathy, but she smiled sweetly. 'Wonderful. I'll do the clearing plan straightaway and give it to you later. Perhaps you could action it in the next couple of days?'

'What will you be doing until then?'

She thought that was a rather strange question. She could have been doing anything private. 'Working in the library, I expect.'

'I don't know if that will be convenient,' Dupont frowned.

'I beg your pardon?' Cathy bristled. This man was a land agent.

'The librarian has an important project to complete.' Dupont seemed deadly serious.

'Goodness. Does Monsieur employ a librarian? That's rather grand. But he didn't tell me about any project. Perhaps I should ask him.' Then she remembered he'd told her that the garden she was to plan had been a pet project. Perhaps he had several on the go?

'Maybe he forgot about it. I wouldn't mention it,' Dupont added.

'Ah, I see,' said Cathy, but she was already wondering what was so secret about the library plan. 'You think I might get in the way?' Dupont looked flustered.

'No, mam'selle. It's just that you might have some problem locating details on the garden. Everything in there is in a mess. And Monsieur likes everything just right.'

'When you see the librarian, perhaps you'll tell her that I'll call round early tomorrow morning and that I won't be getting in her way. Then you can tell me your boss's decision about using the machines. Oh, by the way, I'll walk back. I have lots of things to do.' She shouldered her small rucksack purposefully.

Dupont inclined his head. 'Just as you wish, mam'selle.' He let out a theatrical sigh, then climbed back slowly into the Land Rover. Cathy watched as he started up the engine and took off.

Phew! she thought. He was hard work. He wasn't very welcoming. In fact, I have a shrewd suspicion that I'm putting Dupont's nose out by being here. And, I suspect, he doesn't like hard work. Well, I do!

She wiped her brow. It was getting hot very early today. Suddenly, she was extremely glad that Dupont had decided that a female was not safe in charge of a rotovator. She couldn't imagine managing it in the midday sun.

She took off her jacket. It was hot enough to take off her shirt as well, but she couldn't really do it here, could she? But there was no-one around.

On the other hand, she didn't really want to be bitten by anything, especially mosquitoes and some might be lurking by the water. But then she remembered she'd put on her repellent. She slipped off her top and standing in her vest top, felt a cool breeze tickling her skin.

Stuffing her shirt into the top of her small rucksack and tucking her jeans inside her boots, she made for the silver ribbon of water that fringed the plot. So where was the lake? What a massive place, thought Cathy. She began to walk towards the interesting-looking heap of stone she'd caught sight of straightaway. It resembled a church from a distance, but a very small one. It couldn't be a church. Maybe some kind of monument?

Soon she discovered she was approaching from the rear. For some reason, whoever had built it, had decided that the front should not be seen from the chateau. As she got nearer, she thought it was a folly or maybe a ha-ha.

But she wasn't prepared for the brambles that were attacking its stonework. She made her way carefully round, reminding herself she was so near the edge that she might be stepping in the water any minute. She just had to get out of the bushes as soon as possible. 'Ow!' she cried as a swinging bramble bush encountered her head and tore at her hair.

Next moment, she nearly passed out, not with pain, but shock. A man was confronting her. He must have been working his way round the back. She couldn't run because her stupid hair and the bramble were now inseparable.

'Pardon, mam'selle,' he said. She swallowed desperately as she found herself in close

13

proximity with a hard-muscled naked chest, tanned golden brown. She saw his hand stretch out—to her hair. He was so tall that she had to look right up to see his face. And he was laughing!

His eyes were a mischievous dark brown under a thatch of tousled black, and Cathy felt indignant, confused and horrified all at once as the only thing she could think of at that moment was that she was almost as sparsely dressed as he.

'I'm sorry,' she said in English and watched his eyebrows lift.

'Quiet, please.' He ignored what she said and went on untangling her. It was an extremely difficult situation and he kept on smiling. She felt herself go red.

'Voila!' He had succeeded. Then he picked a twig out of her hair as well.

'Don't!' she said in French, drawing back.

'What were you doing in the brambles? You should have kept your top on,' he said. He was still grinning. She wanted to put her top on but she couldn't. It would be too embarrassing. He was regarding her as if he knew what she was thinking. 'Here,' he said, whipping her shirt out of her knapsack.

'Thank you!' she snapped, slipping it on. 'It isn't funny!' she replied.

'It's very interesting, though.' His eyes were on her body. 'Do you usually go walking through thorn bushes dressed like that? But

14

then—you are English!'

'How dare you? Who are you?'

He shrugged and put his arms up in a typically Gallic gesture. 'I was just going to ask you the same question, mam'selle. I have a right to be here. I work here.'

'So do I!' Cathy retorted.

'That's great!'

'Are you a gardener?' She'd suddenly imagined him doing the rotovating. She blinked.

'Are you a maid?'

'No. I'm a garden designer.'

'Ou, la, la!' The mocking tone annoyed her a lot.

'And I understand everything you say even though I'm English.' Why was she being so defensive? She jerked her head back and, to her chagrin, the bramble struck again.

'Oui, mam'selle, and you are as prickly as these thorns—which seem—to love your hair. Hold still, please.' Next moment, he was picking another one out, that pricked him. He swore. 'Oh, pardon.' And he sucked his finger. 'There. Now, I must get on. I have no more time to rescue damsels who seem intent on their own destruction.'

She winced. He certainly had attitude. 'Get on with what?'

'What I was doing until I heard you scream. Catching my breakfast.' He gestured again, shrugged, turned and disappeared. She peered

15

after him in a daze then followed. It was true. He'd been fishing! There was a rod and basket standing by the water, a small seat, as well as a substantial green waterproof bag from which protruded several large cardboard rolls like the ones which contain posters or maps.

'Want to share the catch?' The man grinned and, pulling out the keep net, proudly produced two large shining fish, thrashing about. Then he put the net back in. She shook her head. 'Well, all the more for me.'

She watched in silence as he packed away his things. She couldn't think of anything to say but her heart was thumping as he turned to the fish in the net. 'Are you going to kill them?'

'Well, I can't eat them alive,' he said.

She turned away to face the front of the building. It was neither a folly nor a church. It was a mausoleum. She could hear thrashing about in the water then silence.

'Grim, isn't it?' he remarked, coming to stand next to her. He had a heavy stick in his hand. The heat from his body connected with hers. 'But I quite like Gothic.'

A moment later he bent down, rolled up the empty net, picked up the basket which she imagined now contained two shining dead fish and shouldered the rod.

'Au revoir, mam'selle.' He gave a tiny, mock bow. 'By the way, I am Luc. I've enjoyed our encounter.'

Cathy blinked. She had enjoyed it, too! Had

he said he was a gardener? She'd be able to find out, she was sure. But why did she want to find out? He was certainly arrogant.

But the meeting had intrigued her. Why shouldn't she find out who he was? Suddenly, Paul came into her head. He'd been handsome, too. And arrogant. Cathy had made a big mistake trusting him.

The sun had gone down now and Cathy felt cold. She buttoned up her shirt and slipped on her jacket. She could find the answer to all her questions back at the house. But Dupont had said that the librarian was engaged on a project and didn't want disturbing. Tough luck, that's her job. I'll kill two birds with one stone. I'll find the old maps of the garden and they're sure to tell me about the mausoleum, she thought. 'And, if she can't be bothered to look, then I'll find out for myself,' said Cathy out loud, picking up her rucksack.

When she'd first visited the chateau, Cathy had wondered if the housekeeper would be as hard going as Dupont. However, although Charlotte was not over-friendly, Cathy sensed, to her relief, that she wasn't resented in the kitchen.

'How's Madame Laine?' had been Charlotte's first inquiry. She evidently liked Marie, which was a good sign and Cathy discovered that she had actually been at the chateau ever since her own mother had played there so many years ago.

The housekeeper also seemed quite intrigued by the idea that Cathy had been asked to do up the wild garden and, soon, they were discussing the planting of herbs and suchlike. Charlotte was a real French countrywoman and a superb cook although Cathy hadn't yet had the opportunity to sample her culinary arts.

The chateau's kitchen was not at all modern but comfortable. It was just the kind of kitchen Cathy would have liked in her dream house. The huge open fireplace and spit remained, as well as several wooden settles. Charlotte told her that the great fire was lit only rarely. Today, they relied on unobtrusive central heating.

'Sometimes at Christmas,' she added, 'we light the fire when Monsieur Bernard is entertaining. His guests like to come down here and get a taste of the atmosphere—as well as the wine. Especially the Americans!'

She indicated the heavy wooden door which led off to Bernard's extensive wine cellars which ran under the floor and ended, Cathy was told, in a series of large caves. It wasn't hard to imagine how the kitchen looked in the winter, she thought, as she placed her ice-cold drink on the massive table. It made her feel hot even to think about it. The temperature that boiling day was at least 30 degrees and perspiration kept running down the side of her face.

She intended to go back to the village and have a lovely, cold shower and tackle the librarian in the afternoon but, at present, she couldn't get her recent encounter out of her head. 'Do you know someone who works here called Luc?' she asked.

'Umm—yes,' replied Charlotte, putting down her own glass. 'Why?'

'I met him by the pool—I mean lake,' Cathy replied. 'He was fishing.'

'Was he?' asked Charlotte.

'He said that he was catching his breakfast.'

'That sounds like him,' said Charlotte. Cathy wished the housekeeper would enlarge on the conversation. She didn't want to be accused of asking too many questions just in case he found out and thought she was interested in him. He was arrogant enough.

'Did he bring them to you to cook?' Cathy thought it would be all right to say that.

'He always throws them back, mam'selle,' was the reply. 'He's very good-natured.'

'Is he?' Cathy could see that Charlotte had a soft spot for him.

'Extremely. Now, would you like another juice?'

'No, thank you. I must go home and have a shower.'

'You look as if you had a rough time down in that garden.' Charlotte smiled knowingly and to Cathy's enormous embarrassment, she felt her face go red. 'Must be all that fishing.'

19

'I don't think so. I don't like killing fish.'

'Pooh, then you won't get on with Monsieur Bernard. He loves blasting away at everything that moves.'

'Oh, dear,' replied Cathy, getting up. 'I'll see you later.'

'You're coming back today then?'

'Yes, I want to meet the librarian.'

'Oh,' replied Charlotte, 'I'm not sure if he'll be here. I don't think he will, actually.'

'Never mind, I'll have a look around the library myself—if that's OK.'

'Of course, mam'selle, anything you like.' Charlotte returned to her task of peeling potatoes. As Cathy left, it occurred to her suddenly that Charlotte had called the librarian 'he'.

Cathy mounted the old bike Marie had lent her, 'Let's hope I get on with him. He's probably about eighty.'

She freewheeled down the drive which was a rather pleasant experience, given that the chateau had been built on a hill. She remembered she hadn't felt that when she'd cycled up though. Now she was having her own back. It was at least half a kilometre to the front gate and the bike's wheels unsettled the white dust of the gravel, sending it into her face as she flew along.

She was just rounding the last corner when she heard the roar of a powerful engine coming towards her. A moment later, a low, grey sports car shot past her, leaving a cloud of dust behind it, causing her to topple on to the verge.

'You fool!' she shouted. 'You nearly killed me!' She stood astraddle her bike, shaking. Then, when she had composed herself, Cathy remounted and wobbled off nervously in the direction of the village.

CHAPTER THREE

'I met someone called Luc today,' Cathy said, as they were just finishing lunch, which in the French tradition had seemed to last for ages. It had been good too; in fact, Marie made every meal matter.

Marie was finishing the last mouthful of her own salad and didn't speak right away, but Cathy could see the twinkle in her eyes. 'Did you say you'd met Luc?'

'Yes, do you know him?'

'I've come across him,' replied Marie, 'but he isn't always at the chateau. I believe he has another job as well.'

'Really?' Cathy couldn't hide her interest. 'What?' Marie shrugged.

'I'm not sure what he does. He's a very versatile, young man. He stays up there in the summer.'

'He was fishing this morning.' Cathy wrinkled her pretty nose. 'He didn't look as if he was working very hard. And he killed the poor fish for his breakfast.'

'That doesn't sound like him,' laughed Marie. 'He's soft really.'

'That's what Charlotte said too. I think you're holding back on me.'

'Well, I've come across him several times in the village and he strikes me as a very nice, young man. What?'

'I think he's patronising,' said Cathy.

'Oh, dear,' replied Marie. 'Why?'

'I was . . . caught in the brambles and he . . . decided to unpick me . . . as well as having a joke at my expense,' retorted Cathy indignantly. Marie giggled, like a little girl. 'I know it sounds funny, but it was his attitude . . .'

'Never mind his attitude. I can see by your face that, whatever you say, you wouldn't mind re-living the experience. Not only is he a nice young man, but he's quite dishy, isn't he?'

'Marie!' said Cathy empathetically, 'I am far too busy thinking about my project to get tangled up with anyone.'

'Even if he looks like Luc?' asked Marie mischievously and Cathy sensed that Marie was very keen on the idea of her finding a new boyfriend.

Once more, in the civilised French tradition, Cathy didn't emerge from her siesta until after three. She'd had her lunch and her shower and now, was ready for battle with the fusty, old librarian. Marie was going shopping so she offered Cathy a lift. In reality, Cathy was grateful as she didn't fancy cycling up the hill again in the afternoon sun.

'If you phone me on my mobile, I'll pick you up,' said Marie as she dropped her off at the top.

'Oh, no, I don't mind coming down on my

own,' replied Cathy, 'and, anyway, it'll be cool then. I intend to stay late and make the most of the daylight.'

As she reached the drive, she gasped. A car was parked in the shade of the courtyard. A smart, grey Porsche, in fact, the same, that had been driven by the psycho, who had almost run her off the road. Cathy snorted. Doubtless he was another of Bernard's friends, but what was he doing here when Bernard was away. Probably sampling the wine!

She wondered whether she was brave enough to let him know quite how close he had come to injuring her, but she realised that such a remark wouldn't be sensible, given her role. Still, she could glare at him if she saw him.

The chateau was a bit like the Sleeping Beauty's castle when she entered. Not a soul stirring. She felt like a peasant interloper as she walked through the hall in her jeans. She should have been gliding along in a ball dress.

She couldn't quite remember where to find the library but, after making a couple of wrong turns, she found the door, opened it and stepped inside. It wasn't huge, but it was very imposing.

The books were all in glass cases, which might present a problem, if she didn't have a key. The cases rose right to the ceiling, but she could see the library steps pulled out as if inviting her to start looking for the old maps of

24

her garden.

She had been used to her bland, college library with its grey, steel stacks and minute cubby holes, where anxious students sat in silence. In contrast, the chateau had a cataloguing system contained in rows of elegant, walnut cases. A computer stood on a desk but, after taking a look, she could see someone had been using it very recently.

She glanced round. But who would give her the keys to the cases? Where were they kept? She got up again and, going over to one of the glass doors, she tried it. Sure enough, it was locked. Of course, it was. The books were probably priceless. Maybe Charlotte knew where they were?

However, there was a door in the corner of the room. It probably led off to the librarian's office. But it was locked too. Grimacing, she remembered that Charlotte had said that the librarian probably wouldn't be there that day.

Tutting with annoyance, Cathy went out of the library and made her way to the kitchen. Charlotte was sitting with a glass of red wine in her hand, while a fresh breeze blew in from the garden through the kitchen door, filling the room with summer fragrances. How civilised, thought Cathy. Wine in the afternoon. Maybe Charlotte had been talking to the mad driver, as another empty glass stood upon the table.

'Oh, you're back,' said Charlotte.

'I said I would be. I suppose you don't know

25

where the keys to the library cases are kept?'

'Probably in the office,' replied the housekeeper.

'How do I get hold of them?'

'You must ask the librarian.' Cathy could see the conversation was getting nowhere.

'But he's not there,' she replied, feeling faintly irritated.

'He is,' insisted Charlotte, 'unless he's gone out again. Is his car in the courtyard?'

'His car?' asked Cathy.

'The sports.'

'Yes. It's there.' Cathy couldn't believe it was a librarian who had almost mown her down.

'Well, he must be there. Knock on his door.'

'Right,' said Cathy, eyes glinting.

'Would you like a glass of wine?'

'Not just now, thank you,' replied Cathy, knowing she sounded like a prim, English miss. 'I've work to do.' She strode across the hall, feeling vengeful. At the moment, no-one seemed to be in the mood to help her.

Once she reached the library, she had cooled down a little. It would be no good alienating the librarian, otherwise she might get nowhere, which now seemed quite likely. She breathed in deeply and decided that she would look up what she wanted and then, she thought indignantly, I'll go and get him out of that office. He's probably drinking himself silly!

26

The next quarter-of-an-hour was taken up by painstakingly making a list of all the books and papers she wanted. And not once did the keeper of the manuscripts appear.

Breathing in deeply again, she stood outside the door and knocked very loudly. Hopefully that will wake him up, she thought. Then she heard quick footsteps.

'Who is it?'

'It's Cathy Murdoch. The garden designer,' she answered loudly. There was a shuffling of papers and a shutting of drawers. 'Yes, I wonder what you've been up to,' she said quietly. A moment later, the door opened and to her disbelief, she was confronted by none other than Luc.

His complete lack of attire beside the pond had been replaced by what Cathy instantly recognised as a light-grey Italian suit and silk tie. He looked—perfect. She blinked. 'What are you doing here?'

'My job,' he replied with a winning smile. 'Come in, mam'selle.' He indicated for her to follow. She was still so surprised that she couldn't move.

'You're the librarian?'

'I am.'

'But I thought you were a . . .' She realised it would be extremely insulting to finish what she was about to say.

'I understand you, mam'selle. But I forgive you.' This speech was delivered so mockingly that Cathy almost exploded.

'But I don't forgive you for nearly killing me at lunchtime.'

His brow furrowed. 'Pardon? I thought I picked you out of the brambles?'

'I mean you nearly ran me over later!' Cathy could hear her voice rising in the most ridiculous, staccato manner.

Even more annoyingly, his response was to laugh, then put a hand on his heart in the most enchanting way. 'I am sorry. I beg your pardon. I do drive too fast sometimes but, you must admit, you were not on the right side of the road.'

'What?' Cathy couldn't remember if she was or was not.

'I think we are both in the wrong. Friends?' He was holding out his hand. She looked at it. She wished that she didn't have to take it, but she couldn't bear not to. His grip was exactly the kind she liked. Warm and strong. They shook hands. 'Now, please come in.' She followed. 'What can I do for you?' He was staring at the slips.

'I . . .' Cathy realised her voice had become a squeak, so she lowered it purposefully. She still had not got over the shock of finding out he was the librarian and, besides, a thousand possibilities of being ensconced with him for a very long time were flooding her mind. 'I would like to see these books . . . and maps, please.' She passed them over. 'I've located the bookcase, but the housekeeper says that you have the key. They're all in the same section,' she explained. He was studying them carefully.

'Oh, dear,' he said, looking up at her from deep, dark eyes. 'I'm afraid I might not be able to help.'

'What do you mean? They're in the catalogue.'

'Yes, but I am sorry I have not had the time to re-catalogue and, these, I think, are some of the oldest items we have . . . and . . . I have a feeling that Monsieur Bernard has been in here and withdrawn many of these titles. I don't know why.'

'But what am I going to do?' Cathy was overcome with disappointment. 'He asked me to plan a new garden and, now, I have no idea where to start. I was hoping to base it on how it looked in the 18th century.'

'What a pity,' said Luc sympathetically. 'Maybe he has kept them in his office. I could go and look for you, but, unfortunately, I have no time today. However, I do know something about the layout of the chateau's gardens. I have studied French history and also the art of landscape and I think that, somewhere in my quarters, I may have some items to help you.'

'In your quarters?'

'Yes, I live up there.' He walked over to the window. She followed him. He pointed to the turreted tower, that was built on to the main part of the house. Her face must have registered astonishment. 'Yes, Monsieur Bernard has been very good to me. As I said, I studied history at the Sorbonne and then went into librarianship and archives. I actually wrote a thesis on the local area in the 18th century and included the chateau in my research. That is how I know Bernard.' He shrugged.

'Very interesting,' she said. He certainly was versatile.

'And how lucky for you, Mam'selle Cathy.' He gave a tiny bow in the manner, which only Frenchmen can carry off.

'Indeed. So what should I do . . . ?' she asked. He might be arrogant concerning his many talents, but he was certainly enchanting.

'I think we must make an assignation.' He smiled and she melted. 'If you would like to come to my tower some time this evening—or tomorrow evening—I would be delighted to discuss your problem further.' Cathy knew what she wanted to do, but she wasn't sure whether she should. However, the words tripped out quite easily.

'Tonight sounds an excellent idea. I do need to get on with my project,' she said, 'but I have to phone my friend first. She is going to come and pick me up, you see. I believe you know her—Marie Laine?'

'Ah, Madame Laine. Yes, a wise lady.' He smiled. At least, now, Cathy had let him know that she wasn't quite alone.

'Is that all right? I'll come back with an

answer soon. May I leave these with you?' She indicated the catalogue slips.

'Of course.'

'Good. I'll see you soon then . . .'

'Au revoir, mam'selle.' She turned and could feel his eyes watching her every move. Cathy's heart was thudding with excitement as she left the library and went outside to phone Marie. She also made sure she was well away from the house when she did.

'Luc has invited you to his tower?' asked Marie. Her voice kept fading, as the signal was poor in the valley and kept breaking up. 'Well, aren't you the lucky one!'

'He's going to help me with the garden project.'

'Oh, sure,' replied Marie. Cathy could tell she was laughing.

'It's true. Marie . . . Did you know he was a historian?' No reply. 'Marie, are you there? He's OK, isn't he? You know what I mean.' Then Marie was back.

'As far as I know, but then I have never been invited to his tower.'

'Did you know he lived here?'

'I told you he comes here in the summer,' said Marie. 'He's an interesting guy, isn't he? Tell you what—if you're scared . . .'

'I am not scared,' retorted Cathy. 'Don't be silly! I know how to look after myself.'

'Fine, but remember I have to answer to your mother. Sorry, only joking. I'll phone you about nine. Just in case he's misbehaving and you want to get away, but I'm sure you won't be finished by then.' Cathy's heart gave a little leap.

'I'll be back by half-eleven.'

'Well done. Can't wait to hear your news. 'Bye.' Then Marie was gone.

CHAPTER FOUR

'How do I look?' Cathy asked, appearing at the door of the lounge. Marie looked up and smiled involuntarily. 'Do you think this is about right?' She gestured to the silk top and evening pants. It had been a very hard choice to make. She didn't want to look over-dressed, nor under. So she'd had to aim somewhere in between.

Cathy was used to wearing jeans and tops most of the time. She and Paul had hardly ever dressed up for anything and she wasn't sure what Luc would expect. She'd only brought one dressy outfit with her and, when she'd looked in the mirror, she'd decided it was fine, but now she wasn't so sure. And Marie was still smiling!

'Go on, tell me!'

'You look wonderful. In fact, you're so much like Rosaline, I could weep. He'll love you, believe me,' said Marie. 'Have you a wrap though? The nights here can be very cold.'

'I don't think I'll be out that late,' laughed Cathy.

'Better safe than sorry. Wait a minute,' replied Marie, walking out of the room to return in a couple of minutes, carrying an exquisite, white, cashmere pashmina. She handed it to Cathy. 'Now, I'll go and get the car out.'

'Oh, do you mind? You're so good to me,' said Cathy.

'Well, you can't go up to the chateau on your bike, can you?' retorted Marie. As they went out of the door into the garden, Cathy heard a night bird singing and smelled roses all around her. Once again, she had the impression she had walked right into a fairy tale.

The feeling lingered and, then, later, gave way to a racing heart as, finally, Marie swung her little car round in the courtyard of the chateau, coming to a halt beside the sleek sports. 'Good luck then,' she said. 'Have a lovely time. And, remember, I'll ring you.'

As she drove off, a black-suited figure appeared at the heavy door of the turret. Cathy breathed a sigh of relief when she saw him coming towards her. Luc had dressed up too. He was wearing a light-grey suit—definitely Italian—and an open-necked shirt. Once again, he looked just right. She was so glad she hadn't come in jeans.

'You look beautiful,' he said simply.

'Thank you.' Cathy's heart was thudding, as he touched her arm.

'This way.' He gestured upwards. 'I'm afraid it's quite a narrow climb. Can you manage in those?' He was staring at her sandals.

'I hope so. I never thought!' replied Cathy grimacing.

'One hundred and fifty steps and no lift. It keeps me fit though.' She was entirely conscious of his presence behind her, as they toiled upwards.

After what seemed an age, they reached a narrow landing, off which led a long, curving corridor, that must have encircled the tower. 'I'll go in front now,' he added. As he passed her in the narrow space, she felt the heat from his body, which made her feel a little dizzy.

The side of the corridor to her right must have been divided into several rooms, which you couldn't see into, because heavy curtains were drawn behind the glass; but the side on the outside, which led along the wall of the turret, was quite daunting. There were slits of windows, that made you realise just how high up you were.

'Look through here,' he said, pausing at one opening, 'I have the best view of the chateau.' It was true. She could see a panorama of the Beniot estate and, over the trees, she also had a bird's eye view of the Castle of Chinon. She was acutely conscious of their two bodies together in such a confined space.

'I wonder if you can see Marie's house,' she asked quietly. She wasn't too keen on heights and, again, just for one moment, she felt a little dizzy. He must have been extremely perceptive, because he caught her arm and held it gently.

'Probably,' he answered. 'I have a telescope,

so we'll have a look later on, shall we?' Then he led her into a room off the corridor.

Cathy's eyes took everything in. It was a room right out of a storybook. The stone walls were curved and hung with several tapestries depicting hunting scenes. The furniture fitted admirably; antique pieces made from a dark, foreign wood that was most likely ebony. Probably bought by some Benoit ancestor from the French colonies.

Two comfortable-looking leather settees were clustered about the ornate fireplace in which had been set a great vase of artificial flowers. Between these was set a large, low table, that was overflowing with books and maps. Luc had really meant what he said then. He intended to show her the old plans of the garden.

He was evidently following her delighted eyes. 'Not a bad, old place, is it, but it doesn't have enough room really.'

'You never stay in the chateau itself then?' she asked.

'No, that wouldn't do. Monsieur Benoit has plenty of his own friends and, after all, I am not his guest.' He sounded quite serious. Of course he wasn't.

'Still, it's a great pad for an employee,' she said. He nodded. 'I'd be happy with it.'

'Would you?' he asked.

'Yes, but look at it.' She gestured. 'It reminds me of the turret at Usse.'

'Ah, the Sleeping Beauty Castle,' he said.

'You know it.'

'Of course. But I'm afraid I have no princess to wake up with a kiss.' She'd been asking for that, she supposed.

'OK, when we've finished all this,' he gestured the maps, 'I'll take you into Chinon and we'll have some food. What do you think?'

'I'd like that.' She felt a little stupid. What had she been expecting? That he'd fall at her feet? She remembered that Marie was going to ring to make sure she was all right. She smiled inwardly. There was no need for concern. He intended to be the perfect gentleman. After all, they were two business colleagues. Suddenly, she was angry that she felt hugely disappointed.

'But that's not to say we can't have a drink while we're working,' said Luc, crossing the chamber to another door, which must have led farther on down the corridor. She watched and saw him open a low cupboard. That must have been the kitchen. 'White or red?' he asked, producing two bottles and showing her.

'Red, I think. But only one.'

'Fine.' He smiled. She noted how expertly he opened the bottle and poured it into two fine glasses and carried it on a tray, which he set on the sideboard. 'Here you are. Hope you like it. It's a good vintage.' Like all Frenchmen, he knew about wines.

'I'm sure I will.' As he handed her the glass, his warm fingers touched hers and she felt a tiny shock. 'May I have a look at these?' she asked to cover her confusion. She walked over to the table.

'Of course. Please sit down.' She did and he sat opposite, his dark eyes caressing her. 'I dug out as much as I could.'

She was turning over the pages quietly. It wasn't like Cathy not to look people straight in the eye, but Luc was having too much of an effect on her.

Suddenly, she realised she didn't want to acknowledge his admiration and show how much she liked him, because she didn't want to get hurt again.

'I can't see much about my piece of land,' she said. 'I'm really quite desperate to get started, but I don't think Dupont is.' She grimaced. 'By the look of it, he didn't want to know when I asked about having it cleared.'

'Oh, trust Dupont,' he replied lightly. 'But he's not all bad. He's a good manager. Now, your plot.' He indicated a heavy volume and opened it at a marker. 'Look. It's mentioned but, as I told you, I didn't think I had anything. But what I do have, I've brought.' He came round and sat beside her, making her heart flutter at his nearness. 'This is the eighteenth century layout of the front and rear gardens, as well as the kitchen garden area . . . Pardon.'

He brushed against her as he opened the map. She scanned it carefully, trying not to think about his nearness . . .

'I can see the river. But where's the lake—and the pool? Were they made when this was drawn?' He didn't answer. She bent down conscious of his face near hers. 'Could that be the mausoleum?'

She stared at an indeterminate dot.

'You're interested in the mausoleum? Was that why you were there, the morning I rescued you?' His eyes twinkled mischievously.

Cathy took a deep breath. 'I'm not particularly interested, but after you left with the fish, I decided to have a closer look.'

A brief frown flitted across his face, which puzzled her. 'And?' He was waiting.

'It's a little spooky.' She smiled.

'Spooky?'

'Well, it is a tomb—but what was very strange was that—it looked as if someone had been inside recently. There hasn't been a funeral, has there?'

Luc raised his eyebrows and grimaced. 'Not to my knowledge. Bernard seems very well,' was his flippant reply.

'No relations died?'

He shook his head. 'I am not aware of his family connections,' he shrugged. He finished his glass of wine. 'More?' She shook her head. He evidently didn't want to talk about the mausoleum.

'When was it built?' Cathy persisted. 'You said something about liking Gothic?'

'Did I? It is very old, but how old, I don't know.'

'Really?' She wanted to say, Well, you should. You're the librarian, but she didn't. However, for some reason, she had a strange feeling that Luc was holding out on her.

'What about this then?' He swiftly changed the subject and handed her a calf-leather volume, bound with gold leaf. 'It's a very detailed book, written by one of the Benoit family, listing all the flora in the gardens. As a gardener, surely this must be interesting to you? Listen to this.' He began to read. After, he showed her lots of other maps and talked about the layout of the chateau. He seemed to know all about it and could make even the dullest subject interesting.

He and she were certainly on the same wavelength. They chatted about him being a historian before he'd been a librarian and which era he had concentrated on, then about her college course and the differences between France and England. And her project wasn't mentioned again until she reminded him. 'I'd like to look at these again.'

'You mean on your own?'

'If you don't mind.'

'Then I shall take them back to the library, so you can pore over them at your leisure.'

'Thank you. And you'll try and locate the

other maps for me?'

'I'll try but, as I said, they are probably in Bernard's possession. I think they will be unobtainable.' He said the word as if it was final. Cathy was almost sure now that he was trying to put her off seeing them. But why? All she really wanted was to study her piece of land and see how it looked in the eighteenth century, so that she could reproduce it; at least, in some small way.

She flipped through another book, then looked straight at him and said directly, 'I've really loved getting to know you, Luc, but I do need to see a map of my piece of the garden and, also, I'd like to find out why Bernard has let it go so much. It seems very strange, given all the effort that has been put into making the rest of the estate so perfect.'

'I'm afraid I can't help you there,' he said. 'I have brought down all I could. You may look at them again in the library, if you wish. I may have missed something. As I said before, I am new to cataloguing. But, after all, perhaps, I am not a very good librarian.'

Cathy was startled at such an admission. He'd seemed supremely in control of everything and, suddenly, here he was, admitting that he wasn't perfect.

He gestured to the books and maps. 'Is there anything else you would like to study here? Or would you like to come and have a look through my telescope at the real thing?'

'I'll settle for the real thing,' she replied. 'Will I be able to see the mausoleum?'

'This is very powerful. I am also what you call a stargazer. I find the stars very beautiful—amongst other things.' He was looking at her so directly, she almost blushed. She stretched out her hand to take the telescope, and he took her hand instead and led her out of the room to the dizzy drop over the castle wall.

'The stars or the mausoleum?' he asked quizzically. What else would she choose? It was not quite dark and the clear, night sky, was studded with twinkling lights while, below, the town clustered like a heap of sparkling jewels.

Luc showed her how to work the apparatus and soon he was whispering the stars' names, as she asked questions. He knew so much about the heavens. It was an entirely magical experience. She could feel his warm breath on her neck and, once or twice, he slipped an arm around her shoulders to steady her.

'Have you had enough?' He was about to close the telescope.

'No, please, could I look at my piece of garden? And the mausoleum?'

'You can try,' he said, 'but you won't be able to pick them out in the dark.' He was right. 'Are you hungry?'

'Yes, I suppose so,' she laughed.

'Well, let's go.' She'd quite forgotten what

time it was. Had Marie rung? They went back inside and she picked up her bag and withdrew her mobile phone. One missed call and one message. *Guess you're OK and having a great time.* Suddenly, she didn't know what kind of time she was having. And it was all her fault. If only she could let go of the past . . .

'I didn't hear anyone call,' he said. He had picked up her wrap.

'No, I had it on silent.' She shook her head. 'It was Marie, wanting to know if I needed a lift.'

'I'm sure Madame Laine understands,' replied Luc. 'I presumed we'd be eating, so I've booked a table in town.'

'How lovely. Thank you,' she said, letting him put the wrap about her shoulders.

The square in Chinon was a tourist attraction in summer and Cathy could understand why. It was surrounded by pretty restaurants, most of which had tables outside, decorated in different colours. The scent of flowers hung in the air, floating off great swathes of roses and lilies, which had been planted in a marvellous array of pots of all shapes and sizes.

Their table was protected by a striped awning and hidden from the public view by another great swathe of flowers. They had sat there for two hours, eating one gourmet course after another and enjoying each other's company.

43

Cathy felt dazzled by Luc's attention and felt quite relaxed after the meal and the wine. 'Thank you so much for bringing me here,' she said sincerely. 'It's so beautiful.'

'I'm glad you like it,' he replied quietly. They still had not spoken of anything particularly personal, except she'd found out that he was an only child; his father was dead and his mother lived in Paris, where he'd attended university. He'd never mentioned if there had been any girls in his life.

On the other hand, Cathy had been quite honest about her situation. She told him briefly about Paul and why she had come to France to get away and clear her head. She also made sure to make it clear that the garden of the chateau was immensely important as she wanted to get it right.

'You will,' he said. 'I've complete confidence in you.'

'How can you have that?' He laughed. 'You don't know anything about my work.'

'I know what you've told me,' he replied, fingering his glass thoughtfully. 'Your enthusiasm is evident. I wish I had some left.'

'I don't understand.'

'Let's say that I lost mine some years ago.' His dark eyes were morose.

'You mean when your father died?' she asked tentatively. Luc nodded.

'It was then I found out who were my friends.' He shrugged. 'But it is far too painful to discuss.'

He looked at his watch. 'It's very late.' Indeed, the square was almost empty.

'No, how could I be! It's all been . . . wonderful.' Which was true, but her heart was beating very fast.

'I'm glad, but now I have to take you home.'

'I only live over there, as you know,' she gestured. 'We could walk.'

They strolled away from the restaurant through streets, that were no longer full of tourists.

She glanced at him briefly, wondering how he felt and he caught her look and smiled as if to say, I understand perfectly, but she knew that, soon, she would be back to reality.

They sauntered on along the wide pavements towards the floodlit statue of the poet, Rabelais. It was as if neither of them wanted the night to be over.

'I can't tell you how much this night has meant to me,' said Luc. He turned to her and, next moment, she was in his arms. Then he kissed her gently. 'Thank you, Cathy.' She felt dizzy with pleasure. They stood together for a moment, then broke apart. 'Come. I'll take you home.'

Cathy didn't know what she expected to happen next, but soon they were standing before Marie's front door. She was trying to decide what to do. Was she ready yet for another relationship? His sensitive eyes were searching her face. 'I'd like to ask you in for coffee, but Marie . . .' She hated making excuses. Would he think she was naive?

'Don't worry, Cathy. I have to get back.'

The house was silent, as Cathy crept about inside, not wanting to wake Marie. She knew she was too strung-up to go straight to sleep, so she went into the kitchen, where she found the note next to the kettle. *If you come back, I hope you had a wonderful time.*

Marie was eating a breakfast of croissants and coffee, when Cathy descended. 'Well,' she said, her eyes twinkling in a most worldly way, 'you must have had a good time. I came in earlier with some coffee for you, but you were fast asleep. Did he say he liked your dress? Where did you eat?'

As Cathy answered, she didn't resent Marie's questions, like she would have her mother's. Her friend gave you the feeling that everything you did was OK with her; that she would understand anything you wanted to tell her.

'So . . . was it good?'

'It was very good,' confessed Cathy. She breathed in deeply. 'Oh, Marie . . . I . . . I like him a lot.'

'I know,' replied Marie wisely. 'Luc is personable, charming and he knows how to treat a girl.'

'Yes, you told me that before.' However much Cathy liked Marie, she was finding this

46

all very irritating. 'You seem to know an awful lot about him, Marie?'

'Only what I see and hear. Inside, he is sensitive, although, on such a short acquaintance, you may not have noticed.'

'I did actually, but how do you know?'

'As I told you, Luc has been coming to Bernard's for some time now. I go up to the chateau as much as I always did, and we talk, when he's around. It's always been a custom in France that young men confide in older women.' Marie leaned back in her chair.

'Marie!' Cathy was a little shocked, although she knew it was true.

'Don't be put out, dear, I am old enough to be his mother. It's purely platonic!' Marie laughed. 'I think Luc would suit you very well as a boyfriend, but one word of warning, he is very preoccupied at the moment with his work, and whether he has time to throw himself into a relationship right now, I'm not certain,' added Marie.

'What is he worried about?' Cathy did indeed feel a little put out. It's never nice when you don't know what someone else does.

'I'm unaware of the particulars. But I can sense that this summer has been a particularly bad time for him personally.'

'What are you trying to say, Marie?' asked Cathy.

'You don't want to get hurt again. I don't think you will but, just in case, if I were you, I would concentrate on that garden of yours instead.'

An awkward silence ensued as the two of them thought about what had been said.

CHAPTER FIVE

Cathy felt a tiny stab of disappointment as she parked her bike. No sign of the Porsche. Luc wasn't there. And he'd said he would be.

It was still very hot; in fact, France was enjoying the kind of heatwave, that caused forest fires in the South and made anyone, who had to work, wish he or she had nothing to do. That lunchtime—for it was almost that when Cathy arrived—the air was thick and cloying, making Cathy wipe her brow several times as she walked towards the plot at the end of the estate.

As she walked, she tried to put last night out of her mind and think of the garden. She had an idea at least how she was going to tackle it, even though she wasn't in possession of the maps that showed how it had looked in the past. The other historic documents Luc had shown her had been enough at the moment to spark off an idea. Once the plot was cleared, she would draw a design that would be very near to what she believed the garden must have looked like in the 18th century.

As the pool came into view, she was very surprised to hear the sound of machinery and her excitement increased. Dupont must have started work!

Two big yellow machines were hard at work,

their sweating drivers stripped to the waist. They must have started early as they had already taken off the top soil and great heaps of the carnage they had created amongst the tangled grasses, trees and thorns, lay piled on the broad, flat ground.

One of the machines drew near to her and she called out to the driver. 'Well done!' He nodded back without the slightest recognition. She ran up to the machine. 'Will you thank Monsieur Dupont for me?' The man shrugged rudely. She could see that he still didn't know who she was. 'Could you stop for a moment?' He pulled up grudgingly. 'What did he tell you?'

'Dupont said nothing, mam'selle. Monsieur Luc gave me my instructions.'

'Monsieur Luc? But what does he know about it?'

'He said I have to get this finished today, mam'selle.' He gestured towards the rubble and brambles. A moment later, the workman roared off again, leaving Cathy standing.

Just who was Luc to command the workers? He must be very thick with Dupont—and Bernard, thought Cathy, turning away. She noticed then that they hadn't touched any of the thicket around the mausoleum, but they were probably waiting to the end for that.

The whole thing was so strange. It was as if Luc was the master of the chateau, when Bernard wasn't there. She shook her head thoughtfully and frowned. She was going to ask him when he came back. But right now, she had to get over to the library, sit down and start her planning.

Cathy wiped the perspiration away, which was running down her forehead profusely and looked over the water longingly. She'd have loved to have dived in to cool off.

The chateau was completely still when she entered, as if no-one had ever used its many rooms. She glanced upwards where the grand staircase led to a gracious landing, off which were a series of rooms, leading to what must be just as elegant bedrooms or suites.

She wondered what it was like upstairs but, of course, there was little likelihood of her being invited to visit. Maybe Marie and her own mother had played up there as children? Then her mind strayed back to her evening with Luc. At least, she knew what the tower looked like.

She had not even been allowed to see the downstairs rooms, except the library. She realised that two reception rooms or salles graced the bottom floor, twins that looked out on to the gardens, but there appeared to be another room, slightly raised above floor level, which must have had a marvellous view.

However, the shutters had been closed to prying eyes, when she had stowed her bike behind a clump of creeper to guard it from the sun and walked along the front terrace.

Perhaps Bernard would treat her to a guided tour when he came back?

She sighed, thinking of the bookwork ahead. She'd had more than enough of that during her examination schedule. Then she cheered up. This was only part of the project and was as important as the rest. Without a proper plan, she couldn't start on the garden. At that moment, she caught sight of herself in an enormous mirror.

She did look scruffy! Hardly recognisable for the sophisticated girl she had been last night. But she was sure Luc would understand she had been working hard in the garden. So, smoothing down her hair and clothes, she found her way to the library again.

Around three, Cathy was getting down to work. She had been disappointed at first, as there was no sign of him.

The little stock room, where she'd met him for the second time, was locked and the elegant shutters in the main library had been carefully closed and bolted, until she went over and opened up the windows behind.

The white wood shutters, scrolled with squares of gold paint kept the room airy, without being stuffy. The library was like a cool cave, scented with the peculiar but unmistakable smell of thousands of old books.

'Oh, great!' she said. Luc hadn't forgotten. He had placed the books and maps they'd been looking at the night before, in readiness for her. However, she needed to switch on one of the brass reading lights to examine them properly.

She settled down but, all the time she was searching for what she needed, she was wondering where Luc had gone. Fishing probably!

Cathy sighed and brought herself back to the task in hand. She was really behaving quite unforgivably, especially as she had been handed her first commission on a plate!

She opened the map that had indicated the mausoleum and tried to concentrate on the point. But then she was thinking of Luc again. Maybe he'd been the one, who'd visited recently. But why? He'd been non-committal when she'd asked him. Well, it's certainly a point of reference, Cathy decided. It could take the place of a grotto in her plan. It would be a bit macabre, but as it was turned towards the pool, that wouldn't matter. The angels were perfect.

She could even surround the mausoleum with a ha-ha; a lovely deep ditch that would keep people and animals away from the mausoleum. The French called this a saut de loup; in English, 'a wolf's jump'. Then, visitors could walk round it and suddenly discover a dear, little, sham bridge constructed on the other side, leading to the angels. It certainly would be half-Gothic. Which set her thinking about Luc again . . .

To balance the wilderness, she'd decided upon a formal layout in the French style for the rest of the ground. He would probably go along with that too, given the look of the rest of the estate.

She felt she was getting on very well but, by now, she was desperately thirsty and, not being able to get into the stock room, she decided to go to the kitchen and find Charlotte who, doubtless, would ply her with ice-cold lemonade.

Pushing her chair back, Cathy left the library and began to make way towards the kitchen along the corridor, her rubber-soled boots making no noise on the worn, stone floor.

The corridor itself was quite dark and lined with classical busts, which looked ghostly from a distance, interspersed by maps and other curios collected from far away places by generations of Benoits. It was also so cool, that it bordered on cold. Goodness knows what this place is like in the winter, thought Cathy, stopping to pull on her light sweater.

Then she heard voices, not coming directly towards her, but echoing around at the end of the corridor. 'Good, Charlotte's here,' she said and quickened her steps. However, when she came out into the back hall, she could see no-one, but she could still hear talking, but this time, in the distance. The back hall had several doors leading off, two of which were ajar, but the buzz seemed to be coming from the one that was closed.

Cathy hesitated. It would not be good manners to burst in on someone's private conversation, but she was sure now that one voice was Charlotte's. She was certain that she wouldn't mind being interrupted for a moment. Turning the handle a little bit, Cathy peeped through. She was right! Charlotte was talking to someone.

Luc didn't appear his usual cool suited self. Instead, he was dressed in a simple black collarless shirt and jeans.

Just as Cathy was about to open the door, her sixth sense told her to wait. She wasn't sure why, but the way they were conversing seemed not only urgent, but secretive. Cathy felt like an interloper; as if she knew that she should not be observing the couple. They were talking rapidly in French.

'Are you sure it's all right, monsieur?' Charlotte asked. Luc leaned towards her, almost as a conspirator would.

'I'll make sure you are not involved, Charlotte,' he replied, taking her by the arm familiarly and leading her out of sight. Cathy couldn't help but open the door a tiny bit wider to see where they had gone.

The two of them were standing in front of a magnificent door, inlaid with different woods and Charlotte was holding out her bunch of keys.

'Don't worry, Charlotte,' Luc said, as he took the keys from her and turned one in the lock. 'You go back to the kitchen. Are you sure no-one else is in the house?' Charlotte nodded.

Cathy gasped. What were the two of them up to? Of course, they didn't know she was there. She hadn't bothered to present herself to Charlotte earlier. She grimaced. She had to find out what Luc was doing. Where was his car? It was blatantly obvious he didn't want anyone to know he was in the house either. Disappointment hit her. He'd said he'd been looking forward to seeing her. He'd forgotten that quite easily!

When Cathy was upset, she did silly things. She watched Charlotte walk away and, several moments later, found herself outside the massive door, which was not completely shut. She breathed in deeply and pushed the handle a little, without thinking what would happen if she was discovered. But she had to find out what Luc was up to. She couldn't have borne it, if she hadn't.

Peering round, her heart thumping alarmingly, she glimpsed Luc. He was sitting in the gloom with his back to her, behind a massive antique desk, that must have looked out through the magnificent window on to the front of the chateau. That's the one I noticed with the shutters down, thought Cathy.

Suddenly, she realised what he was doing

and watched with horror as he attempted to open one drawer after another. He had a small tool, which was evidently up to the task as he managed to pick each lock successfully and rifle through the papers within.

Cathy couldn't believe it. Was Luc a common burglar? She'd also realised that this must be Bernard's private study as, between the elegant bookshelves full of files and boxes, it was lined with portraits of his ancestors, who looked sternly down at the wrongdoer below.

Cathy felt sick now at this demonstration of infidelity. Here were Bernards' two trusted employees behaving in the most reprehensible manner. But what was Luc looking for? She remembered wryly that he'd said Bernard had all the old maps she wanted and that he couldn't obtain them as they were locked in the study. What a liar! thought Cathy grimly, and I was taken in by him. That was what hurt!

She almost gasped out loud then, as Luc jumped up, empty-handed—he'd evidently drawn a blank—and hurried over to the wall by the great stone fireplace that was even taller than he was. Taking a library stool, he climbed on it and, to Cathy's amazement, started pressing around the wall hurriedly.

A moment later, part of the wall slid aside and Cathy found herself staring at a great safe. He was going to break into it! She couldn't bear it. What was he doing? Tears started in her eyes. She knew they were from anger and disappointment. But what was she going to do?

She had absolutely no idea. Who should she tell? Marie? The police? Or should she confront Luc and see if he had an explanation. But he was so plausible that she'd probably believe it. It would have to be Bernard. But he was in New York. No, she was going to have to go on as normal and wait for him to return. That seemed the most sensible thing at the moment.

CHAPTER SIX

Charlotte was sitting in the kitchen with a glass of wine in front of her. Probably trying to calm her nerves. She turned as Cathy entered and there was a fleeting expression of unease in her eyes. Or so Cathy imagined.

'You're here?' Charlotte said.

'Yes, I've been here quite a long time,' replied Cathy.

'Inside?' Cathy knew Charlotte was probing, so she was going to play her at her own game. The monstrosity of what the two of them were up to almost choked her yet, inside, that little voice of emotion was telling her that there might be a good reason for what Luc was doing.

'In the library. Working. And I was so thirsty, I thought that I'd come and ask you if there was any lemonade.'

Instead of offering her anything straightaway, Charlotte's response was another echo of her guilt. 'How long have you been working in there?'

Cathy wasn't going to give anything away. In fact, she wanted to make the housekeeper squirm. 'Quite a long time. It's surprising how you can concentrate when you find something that surprises you.'

'Surprises you?' asked Charlotte.

59

'Um,' replied Cathy nodding. She saw the housekeeper's outward calm dissipate a little. 'Isn't Luc around today?'

'Oh, I don't think so,' replied Charlotte and, a moment later, changed the subject very neatly with, 'Would you care for a glass of wine? I've had it in the fridge.'

'Great,' she smiled, but she really wanted to shout, Liar. She took the glass and sat down at the table. Charlotte wasn't going to be let off that easily and, when Luc had finished his root around in someone else's property, maybe he'd come in too.

Cathy grimly sipped the wine, making it last as long as she could, but he didn't appear. Charlotte didn't speak either and the atmosphere was thick with unspoken questions. Cathy put down her glass finally. The wine seemed to have gone straight to her head and she felt reckless. 'That was lovely.'

'More?' offered the housekeeper. The little voice of reason was warning her now. Keep quiet. Don't let her know you know.

'No, thank you,' replied Cathy. 'I've work to do. By the way, that shuttered room at the front of the house. Is it an extra reception room? It looks very interesting.' She knew she was being devious and cruel, but she felt angry at the two of them for deceiving her.

'Why do you ask?'

'I saw it as I walked along the terrace. I left my bike behind the creepers to shade it from the sun.'

'This morning?' Cathy couldn't miss the tiny note of alarm in the reply.

'I can't remember quite when. No, it must have been this afternoon.'

'Monsieur orders the shutters to be always pulled. It is his study and it holds many valuable items.' Charlotte's voice was brusque and cold.

'I see. Of course, these days anywhere is likely to be burgled.' Cathy realised she had gone almost too far.

'That is true, mam'selle.'

Cathy made her way back. She still couldn't bear the thought that she had been attracted to someone else, who couldn't be trusted. She felt awful; as if she had been betrayed.

To her astonishment, the door to the stock room was ajar. She hesitated, then approached it gingerly, trying to compose herself so that— if Luc was in there—he wouldn't know she had seen what he'd been doing. It wasn't going to be easy, but she had to manage it.

Luc was sitting in the small, cramped room, with his back to her. He was reading. It wouldn't be right to creep up on him, but she would have liked to, so she could see what he was doing. Then reason overtook anger. No, she was more likely to find out what he'd been up to, if she took it slowly. Charlotte was bound to tell him about their conversation, seeing they were so thick with each other.

'Luc,' she said quietly. He jumped, then spun round in the office chair. His smile was as marvellous as ever.

'Cathy! I've been wondering how long you'd be.' He jumped up and to her utter consternation, kissed her on both cheeks familiarly.

'I've been here for some time actually,' she replied, but the answer didn't seem to faze him.

'Yes, I could see you've found the material I left out,' he answered coolly. 'Was it any good?'

'It was,' she replied. 'I discovered several things I never knew before.' But her double meaning didn't seem to hit home. 'How about you? Where have you been?'

He shrugged. 'Out and about,' he answered, looking at his watch. 'What a pity it is too late for us to have lunch together. Perhaps tomorrow?'

'Perhaps.'

'Is something the matter? Have I upset you?' He looked a little puzzled, then he laid his hand softly on her arm. She almost trembled at his touch.

'No, you haven't,' she lied, 'but now I've started on the books, I won't have much time for socialising.' He was regarding her quizzically. He took her hand and she let it lie in his.

'Now I know I have done something wrong,

Cathy, but what?'

She wanted to scream it out then; that he was a crook; that she'd seen him cracking a safe, but she didn't. What she was feeling now was more sorry than angry.

'Please tell me. Was it something I said last night?' He seemed genuinely sincere.

'No, last night was great. You haven't done anything. It's just me—how I feel at present,' she answered lamely.

'Ah, les femmes,' he replied maddeningly, as if to imply women were apt to change their mind at a whim. 'So . . . you want to get on with your work. OK. Then I shall get on with mine. If you want me, you know where I am. And, of course, if you change your mind, the invitation is still open.'

'I'll see.' Cathy had heard of people saying their hearts ached. Hers really did. 'Are you working on something interesting?'

'Just some papers. Quite boring really. Not nearly as interesting as yours.' He smiled again, but something else in his eyes told her that he wasn't happy. At that very moment, the telephone on his desk rang. He picked it up quickly. 'Yes?' Then covered the receiver and mouthed, 'Sorry,' to her.

Cathy who would have dearly liked to eavesdrop, withdrew, closing the door behind her.

'Damn!' she said out loud and retreated to her desk, but her mind wasn't on anything except what she had seen and heard. Five minutes later, she was folding up the maps and closing the books. There was no way she could just sit there with him next door.

As she was about to leave and wondering whether she ought to say goodbye, his door opened. Every time she saw him he looked more handsome, but since she had watched him rifling Bernard's study, that was the only image that stayed in her mind.

'I'm sorry, but it was an important phone call.'

'That's OK.'

'Are you going? I thought you had a lot of work to do.' He was looking at the table.

'I changed my mind. I'm not in the mood.'

'That's a pity. Instead of lunch tomorrow, we could have had some tea. Like the British do.'

'It's a bit hot for tea,' replied Cathy, wondering what was coming next.

'Perhaps you prefer lemonade. Charlotte makes it divinely. Why don't we both go to the kitchen?' Cathy suddenly realised who'd been on the phone. Charlotte. Who must have told him. Now he knew. Suddenly, Cathy went cold.

'No, thank you. I'm going back to Marie's. I told her I'd be home early,' Cathy lied. She wasn't exactly afraid, but wary.

'You came on your bike?'

'How did you know that?' asked Cathy.

'I saw it. Under the creeper outside

Bernard's study.' There was no mistake now. Charlotte had told him everything. 'It's extremely hot. Let me take you home in the car.'

'Goodness, no,' replied Cathy. 'Strangely, I didn't see your car when I left the bike.'

'No, I put it in one of the stables to save the paintwork.' He had an answer for everything. 'Please let me take you, Cathy. Then I can make up for whatever I've done.'

'You haven't done anything,' she reiterated. 'I wouldn't hear of you getting the car out. Anyway, I like riding my bike,' she added airily.

As she wheeled out her bike into the blazing afternoon sun, past the reception room windows, she saw that he was still watching as she mounted and wobbled off across the gravel.

'What's happened?' asked Marie. 'I wasn't expecting you back yet.'

'I think the heat's got to me at last,' Cathy lied, collapsing on the settee. In fact, she did feel a little sick. However, before long, she was sipping a long, cold drink, laced with ice.

'I've never heard you complain about the sun before,' said Marie anxiously, putting her hand on Cathy's forehead, as her mother used to. 'Next time, give me a ring and I'll pick you up.' Cathy breathed in deeply, not sure how much to disclose to Marie.

'Luc offered me a lift actually.'

65

'And you didn't take it?'

'He asked me to lunch as well?'

'I thought you liked him!'

'I do . . .' She almost said 'did', but checked herself just in time. 'But I think things were going a little too fast between us.'

'And would that be a bad thing?' asked Marie.

'No, but . . . I think that I'm not ready for another relationship yet,' lied Cathy.

Seconds later, her friend asked, 'What has he done to upset you?' Cathy saw an anxious expression cross Marie's face.

'Nothing particular,' replied Cathy, hating to tell untruths all the time.

'I think he's a very nice person,' said Marie, 'and you could certainly do worse but, as you say, maybe it would be better to concentrate on this work you've decided to take on, although I can't imagine why, when you're meant to be on holiday and relaxing.'

'I like my work and, especially now, I have my very own garden to plan.'

'Oh, well,' Marie smiled, 'doubtless it will all come right. I remember when I was young, I had lots of beaux . . .'

'Including Bernard?' interrupted Cathy.

'He'd have liked it, as I told you when you first met him, but I wasn't keen.' She didn't seem disposed to say any more, so the conversation ended abruptly with, 'Another glass?' Cathy shook her head.

'I think I'm going to go upstairs for a rest, after all.'

Soon, she was lying on top of the bed—it was too hot to be covered—with a silk shade over her eyes to blot out the light. If only she could do the same with the memory of earlier on.

Cathy woke up with a start. She wasn't sure why, but it was probably the delicious smell that was wafting up the stairs. Marie was such a good cook and Cathy hadn't eaten for what seemed like ages. Cathy pulled off the shade and consulted her watch. Nearly six. She'd fallen into a dreamless sleep. Probably from exhaustion.

She lay there in the pretty bedroom, collecting her wits. It was so different here from her small student flat, that was so poky and had become very untidy since Cathy had been involved in her exams. She decided then when she returned, she'd have to clear up properly!

Here, in Marie's home, the white furniture throughout the upstairs rooms gave them all a bright and airy quality. In her bedroom, the décor was the same. Pretty curtains, that matched those at the windows, had been fixed behind the glass doors of the carved armoire that, in itself, was so French.

Cathy sighed. What was she going to do about the crime she'd seen committed with her own eyes? She'd never been in such a position before. She had no experience of such things. She breathed in slowly to calm herself and let the slight breeze, that was coming in from the open window, try to soothe her. After all, what Luc had been doing wasn't really any of her business.

But, then maybe it was. Bernard was her employer and, surely, he ought to know. She didn't like interfering, but cracking someone's private desk and then their safe, was a serious matter.

Perhaps she ought to confront Luc. But could she do it? None of her earlier worries had disappeared. She got up and padded over to the window, which looked out over the orchard and the corner of the house. The sun was very bright and shards of light darted through her head. The ache was nearly gone, but the brightness made her blink. She had forgotten to pull the shutters.

She drew back and sat down in the low armchair. A moment later, she was suddenly conscious of low voices coming from below. Marie had a visitor. Cathy hoped she hadn't invited someone for dinner. The Frenchwoman was notoriously sociable and seemed to be friends with everyone from the mayor down.

'Phew,' said Cathy, 'I'll just have to pull myself together, if she has. After all, it's her house!' She leaned forward and looked through to see if there was a car parked, then jumped back. Although she couldn't see Marie, she could see none other than Luc, positioned at the corner of the building. He must have been talking to Marie, who was evidently standing on the front door step.

Cathy couldn't hear what they were saying from that distance, although by his urgent gesticulations, she could sense the frustration in what he was saying. Marie had a hand on his arm as if trying to calm him down.

She sat back in the chair immediately and, involuntarily, put her hands over her ears to blot out the sound. She'd had enough of eavesdropping. Her heart was beating very fast. What was he doing here?

A tiny stab of hope sprung through her. Perhaps he'd come to see Cathy to explain his behaviour? If only he had, then maybe it would be all right. Maybe Marie had invited Luc to dinner after what Cathy had told her, in the hope they were going to make up?

A moment later, she heard a car door slam. He must have parked outside the gate at the front, instead of driving round to the space at the back. She shelved that explanation idea immediately. No way had he come to explain. Anyway, he'd had the chance before, when they spoke in the stock room. She still wasn't sure that he realised that she'd seen him in Bernard's study, although he probably did.

A horrible thought passed through her mind. Was he discussing with Marie what he'd been up to? Maybe she was in on it? But she wouldn't be! That's a mad idea, she told herself firmly. But you can't help thinking stupid things when you've seen something like that, the reasonable little voice in her head persisted.

She sat for a few moments, miserably trying to work it all out, but, finally, got up and walked dully to the en suite shower, where she allowed the tepid water to soothe her and wash away, for at least a few minutes, the worries, that were besieging her . . .

Cathy didn't feel like dressing up, so she put on a shirt and her cropped jeans. An idea was already forming in her mind . . . When she came downstairs finally, she was both relieved and strangely disappointed.

'You look better!' said Marie. 'I hope you like stew. Moules and such like?'

'I sure do,' said Cathy. 'Can I help?' Marie shook her head.

'No, everything's in hand. Did you have a good sleep?'

'Excellent? Anybody been?' Cathy felt she had to ask, although she hated herself for not trusting Marie. She was sorry when she had.

'No-one of consequence,' said Marie, pausing ladle in hand. 'Why?'

'Nothing. I only wondered.' She hesitated, then walked over to the stove. 'Gosh, that looks scrumptious,' she added to hide her disappointment. Marie was lying to her, but why?

'Hopefully, it is,' said Marie. Cathy's spirits plummeted suddenly. She took a deep breath to calm herself. Why didn't Marie tell her that Luc had been? What was she hiding?

Cathy finished helping Marie clear the table and wash up. Marie only used the dishwasher when she had a dinner party. As she hung up the wet tea cloth, Cathy's idea had now become concrete. She was going to act on it 'I think I'll go for a ride,' she said. 'I've eaten so much.' The garden door was open and it was a wonderfully warm and balmy evening.

'I'd like to come with you?' asked Marie. 'I could do with losing some weight after all that.' She grimaced and patted her tummy.

'You don't need to,' smiled Cathy, even though she didn't feel like it. 'I mean, I'd like to go on my own, if you don't mind. I've a lot to think about.'

'I understand,' Marie nodded. She probably thought that Cathy was still upset about falling out with Luc.

She knew that, although she had wished that she'd never seen Luc doing what he did, nor looking out of the window at Marie and him together, she had. The first experience had been shocking, but the second had already begun to spoil her relationship with Marie, whom she loved, almost as much as her own mother.

Cathy couldn't go on suspecting her. She

could have asked Marie outright, but would she have told her the truth. Anyway, Cathy wanted to hear it from Luc himself.

'Where will you go?' asked Marie.

'Probably I'll ride along the river, or maybe I'll park the bike and take a walk round the town.' She wasn't going to tell Marie where she was really going.

Cathy had decided to ride up to the chateau and surprise him in his tower. If he wasn't there, she'd come back.

Maybe it was a stupid idea, but she didn't want to keep on torturing herself with questions, that she couldn't answer. She had a torch in her bag and her bike had lights. Anyway, she wasn't afraid of the dark, and she wouldn't be that long.

Cycling up to the chateau in the early dusk was quite an experience. Before she left, Cathy had gone upstairs and changed into her full-length jeans, and how glad she was. The air was clouded with midges and she kept riding into great swarms of them, whirling crazily along the country lane, where the trees overhung. She breathed a sigh of relief when she reached the gate to the estate, as the insects evidently didn't like open spaces.

She began thinking what it would be like if she was walking along with Luc. The night when they'd dined had been magical, as well as their walk along the river. She wanted that feeling to return above everything. But she told herself sensibly that it probably never would.

She shook off the thoughts and looked instead at the sweet, summer wild flowers bordering the road, releasing their delicate scent into the air; many you would never find now at home in England. It was a lovely journey and the light would last until ten at least. It was so quiet that she felt, for a while, like the only person left in the world. But then she remembered where she was going and why.

As the hill to the chateau lengthened, she got off her bike and wheeled it along the verge, all the time going over how she was going to approach Luc. She decided that she would ring the bell to his tower and, if he was there, she wouldn't go inside, even if he asked her to.

If he was a crook, like she suspected, he'd probably want to make a quick getaway! Cathy had a good imagination and her mind ran over so many possibilities that she had reached the chateau courtyard on auto pilot and without being careful not to be seen. She parked her bike out of sight and hurried alongside the tower wall.

She glanced up at the turret. There was no way of seeing if there were any lights on, given that Luc's rooms were hidden behind the corridor. Smoothing down her hair, she arrived at the door and, before she could change her mind and go home, she took a deep, firm breath and pressed the bell. She could hear it ring somewhere in the depths, but no-one came down the stairs. She tried again, then let go. Silence.

'He's not in,' she said out loud. 'Why did I think he would be?' She could have cried.

She turned away from the door and looked down the garden. The evening was more than dusky now. Twilight was approaching—a spooky kind of time, when the mist was coming up through the top of the trees and wreathing them in a grey, wispy blanket.

Suddenly, she thought she saw a light in the distance. Her heart leaped. Maybe Luc was in the garden. Should she look? 'Don't be silly, Cathy,' she said. 'It could be anyone.' But it could be Luc! Maybe he'd gone night fishing.

The light was steady for a moment, then as the trees moved in the oncoming night wind, it wavered eerily. 'I know the garden,' she said bravely. 'I'll just go round by the parterres and see if I can see any more from there.'

The flower gardens were at the front of the house, shaped formally and the ones near the hedge were full of heavy-headed roses. She slipped along until she came out at the front and, to her amazement, she saw that the chateau was lit up. In the circular space in front was parked a large, low Citroen. Added to that, the light was on in Bernard's study.

Cathy stopped, her heart beating madly.

Bernard must be back from New York! Hadn't someone said he liked to surprise his staff. It's a good thing he didn't come back earlier, she thought quickly, then corrected herself. What was she thinking of, defending Luc? No! Bernard should have come yesterday when he might have caught his precious librarian opening his private safe.

Now she really didn't know what to do. She still wanted to investigate the light; to see who was out in the garden—maybe it was Bernard. The thought gave her courage.

Without any more hesitation, Cathy hurried through the parterres, watching the light getting brighter all the time. She knew by now where it was. In the area of her garden, near to the water. It was so much easier to get to, since the men had cleared the land. Once or twice she nearly collided with a big heap of earth, which was a tiny bit frightening, but by the time she was half way across, she realised that, in fact, the light was coming from the mausoleum.

Cathy's stomach turned over. After all, it was a tomb. Then she remembered what her grandma used to say, when little Cathy was afraid of seeing a ghost. 'The dead won't hurt you—only the living.'

The men had still not cleared that area around the pond, which gave her the opportunity to make her hurried way through the brambles. It was a path she didn't like, but she was getting used to avoiding the thorns. It was almost dark now and a large, yellow moon was on the ascent. The light was certainly coming from the area of the mausoleum, but not from the place itself.

The Jeep's headlights spread a great pool of brightness on the ground and partially over the dark water. The engine was running and she wondered how she hadn't heard it before. Probably because the night wind was blowing the sound in the opposite direction.

Cathy crept nearer and nearer and then jumped back as she saw them. The land agent, Dupont—and Luc. The latter was muddy, as though he'd been digging and the door to the mausoleum was half open. Dupont looked his usual self, except that he was gesticulating wildly in the direction of the house. Cathy strained to hear the urgent conversation. Then she caught a few snatches. 'You have to get away. He's back!'

'I can't now. I'm almost through!' That was Luc.

'You have to. Now! I'll take you to your car. Shut it up!' She watched in horror as the two men struggled to close the heavy door, while the peaceful angels looked on as if nothing was happening to violate the sacred place they guarded. Cathy's head was whirling. Dupont was in on it too. What was going on? They must all be crooks. All of them. She'd have to tell Bernard!

The men managed to close it up and to stamp out all signs of them being there. Cathy watched dumbly from the shadows. After they had finished, they walked over to the Jeep. Luc's face was pale and defiant in the lights. 'I'm going to finish off what I started,' he said gruffly. 'I haven't spent the last year of my life to be cheated now. I'm coming back tomorrow night.'

'Well, I'm not risking it,' said Dupont. 'I daren't now he's back.'

'No-one's asking you to,' replied Luc. 'You have done enough, mon ami, I could not have expected more. I shan't forget it. Come on then.' With that, Dupont climbed into the driving seat and Luc the other side. A moment later, he was turning the vehicle and driving off, not in the direction of the house, but along a narrow path beside the water.

Cathy leaned against the walls of the mausoleum, her head spinning. What was she going to do? She could go up to the house and tell Bernard everything or she could go home and forget what she'd seen. Whatever secret the mausoleum contained, it seemed as if it was ready to yield it. And Luc, who was a mystery himself, seemed determined to discover it.

CHAPTER SEVEN

'Are you surprised that Bernard has come back,' asked Cathy, as she broke her croissant into her black coffee. She had soon reverted to French habits.

'No,' replied Marie. 'That's what he always does. He says he's going to be away, then he returns in the night unexpectedly to cause confusion. It drives everyone mad.'

'I wonder why,' said Cathy, but Marie didn't appear to notice the slight hint of sarcasm.

'Did you speak to him last night?' she asked.

'No, I thought it was a bit late.' When Cathy had come in, she'd been able to tell Marie about Bernard's return but, naturally, she'd kept quiet about her real errand and what she had overheard Luc and Dupont saying. 'I, for one, am really looking forward to seeing him this morning and showing him my plans for the garden. I hope he likes them.' She was determined to be bright, and to behave as if nothing else had happened; but what had, lay like a leaden lump in the pit of her stomach.

'I expect that you were hoping to see Luc, too?' Cathy could see that Marie was probing. 'I take it he wasn't there last night.'

'I never saw him,' lied Cathy, 'and, anyway, I told you I was cooling it off.'

'I'm not sure I believe you,' smiled Marie,

'but don't be disappointed if you don't see him today either. I heard from Charlotte that he'd planned to go off for a couple of days. Paris, I think. He'll be cross that he's missed Bernard coming home.' Cathy listened dully.

When was this lying going to end? She knew! When she found out what was going on!

'Well, I'll certainly tell Bernard how helpful Luc has been to me in the library,' replied Cathy sweetly. She couldn't help but catch the slight look of anxiety that briefly crossed Marie's face. 'And I shan't be disappointed. Don't worry, Marie.'

'If I were you, I wouldn't mention Luc helping you to Bernard,' said Marie suddenly. 'In fact, I wouldn't mention him at all.'

'Why?' asked Cathy, feigning a puzzled look and trying to keep calm at the same time. She wanted to ask Marie outright what she, Luc and the rest were up to, but something was holding her back. Perhaps the hope that she might be wrong and the relationship that had been built between her family and Marie could be ruined for ever.

'It's just that Bernard doesn't like any of his employees doing extra work, as it were.' It was a lame excuse.

'Well, he offered me Dupont's help.'

'It's different when he offers. Bernard likes to know everything. He doesn't like people going behind his back.'

'I'll bet he doesn't, thought Cathy. The

irony of this conversation was unbelievable.

'But I'd never do that,' she responded.

'You don't want to get Luc into trouble, do you?' frowned Marie. 'He relies on his summer job.'

'Of course I don't. I won't breathe a word about him to Bernard. I'm sure he wouldn't have liked me being invited up to the tower either.'

'I can assure you that he wouldn't,' replied Marie, quite sharply. 'He's very old-fashioned. By the way, while I remember, I have another word of warning. Sorry!' Cathy lifted her eyebrows, wondering how far Marie was prepared to go to protect Luc. 'If you do go out for a ride tonight, I should keep right away from the estate.'

'Why?'

'It was all right before, when he was away, but . . . Bernard has a thing about poachers. One night, he even shot one! He wouldn't check, if it was dark and he caught someone trespassing.'

'No!' Cathy was really shocked. 'That's illegal.'

'Technically, it might be, but Bernard seems . . .' Marie shook her head. ' . . . seems to lose his senses, when he has a gun under his arm.'

'Charlotte told me he's fond of shooting.'

'Too fond as far as I'm concerned. But it's in the blood.'

'How do you mean, Marie?'

'The Benoits hunted boar and deer on the estate—and peasants, before la Revolution. And several of his noble ancestors paid for the latter with their heads.'

'Oh, dear!' grimaced Cathy.

'But the line survived. Whether it will now, of course, is another matter.'

'You mean because Bernard isn't married?'

'Exactly,' said Marie, sitting back in her chair. 'But he's had his chances.'

'Tell me.' Marie looked down and drank some more coffee. 'Please,' pleaded Cathy. She desperately wanted to know more but, then, something in Marie's manner warned her that she shouldn't persist.

'Bernard is a very difficult man. Often, I suspect he is manic,' added Marie.

'Surely not?'

'He's also very shrewd and single-minded, which is a frightening combination. He wants what he wants and he won't stop until he gets it, whatever it is. He has made many enemies. He is very powerful and, if he is crossed, well . . .' Marie shrugged and poured herself some more coffee.

'Maybe I shouldn't have accepted his offer to do the garden,' said Cathy quietly. She wanted to add, Nor seen the things that I have.

'Well, I won't say I told you so, but, never mind, dear, you aren't involved with him in any other way except gardening. He wants that plot doing over and you are the one he chose.

Don't worry, you'll be all right.'

Marie was looking at the kitchen clock. 'I have to hurry. I have a hair appointment in town and then I'm meeting a friend for lunch. Have a good day with Bernard. I'm sure he'll like everything you've done.' Marie patted Cathy's arm. 'There's plenty of food in if you want to pack your lunch. You might be lucky though and Bernard will treat you.

'Don't bother with the washing up. Oh, and if I were you, I'd ring him and say you're on your way. He's quite formal and also extremely busy. Then you'll know whether he can fit you in for a meeting.'

Marie had been right. When Cathy had phoned Bernard, he had told her that he couldn't see her right away, because he had an enormous amount to catch up on, as well as sorting out several important estate matters, that had cropped up in his absence. 'I am sorry, mam'selle,' he'd added, 'but I shall be happy to see you at midday in my study. Charlotte will show you where it is.' As if Cathy didn't know!

So she had taken herself off to her garden, where she had been surprised to see that the men had left. The machines had disappeared and the ground was flat. They had done a good job. Everything had been cleared satisfactorily, except for the tangled undergrowth around the mausoleum.

Who had ordered them to leave that as it

was? Doubtless, Dupont! Why? Probably because he knew that Luc would be coming back that night and needed to be as inconspicuous as possible. However, if Bernard had ordered it to be left as it was, that would scupper Cathy's plans regarding the proposed ha-ha.

Still, she needed his approval for that, as well as everything else, so she started getting her hands dirty by measuring up and making notes as to where new soil would have to be tipped and where she would put this plant or that shrub. She had made a long list of possibilities. She had chosen plants that would look good throughout the year for her little wilderness. She liked ornamental grasses and had found a place for drifts of Pennisetum bordering the pool.

Suddenly, she was imagining herself sitting on the secret seat, kissing Luc, being held in his arms; a thought which she immediately dispelled and erased from her mind. She became so taken up by what she was doing that she forgot everything else, until she glanced at her watch.

She could hardly believe it. She was almost late for her appointment with Bernard, which meant she wouldn't have time to wash, or change into the pretty, summer dress and sandals she'd brought with her purposely for the meeting. She sighed in disgust. She looked like a tramp!

Anyway, if he did ask her to lunch, which she really hoped he wouldn't, she could make some excuse that she wanted to go to a bathroom and effect an immediate change.

Immediately, she thought about Luc and his last invitation, which she'd turned down. Now she wished she'd kept it. For all she knew, she'd never see him again. She realised she should have been glad about it, but somewhere inside, she longed to.

She wanted to make him explain his behaviour and, although she knew she was being childish, somehow she was hoping that when he did, everything would be all right again between them. But, now, it might be too late. Unless, she could find a way to see him again. Of course, she knew where he was going to be that evening. But could she take the chance?

She was thinking of all the possibilities and, especially, if she was daring enough, as she hurried through the gardens in the direction of the chateau. She was also wondering how she was going to talk to Bernard, without constantly thinking of what she'd seen.

Five minutes later, she had retrieved her holdall, from the basket of her bike. The bag held, not only her clothes and shoes, but also her blue print for the new garden. Only a minute late, she was standing outside the study, knocking. She breathed in deeply in response to his curt, 'Come in!' Her hand wavered on the door handle. He didn't sound in a very good temper.

Perhaps he had discovered someone had been going through his desk and had been trying to crack open the safe? Cathy didn't known if Luc had managed it, but if he'd been after money and taken it, then Bernard certainly would have called the police by now . . . Cathy's imagination was running madly over all the possibilities as she walked in, as calmly as her fast-beating heart would allow.

Bernard evidently didn't suspect her of anything, because he was coming round the desk to meet her and a moment later, to her utter discomfiture, he kissed her familiarly on both cheeks.

'Bonjour, Cathy,' he said, 'working hard, I see.' Cathy was certainly looking quite different from the last time he'd seen her. She was acutely conscious of her old cut-off jeans and the simple tee-shirt, with her college motto, which was streaked with soil marks.

She had taken off her gardening boots at the door and was in her socks. She looked down and grimaced. At least she'd had time to comb through her hair, which fell glossy and shining on to her shoulders.

'Sorry for this,' she apologised.

'No, on the contrary, it is a change to see someone dressed as they should be for work. Please, sit down,' he said, smiling but, as she had noticed at the dinner party the first time

85

she'd met him, the smile didn't seem to reach to his eyes. It was as if his mind was far away somewhere, calculating the next speech or task. 'How are you getting on? I see that the plot has been cleared.' So he had been down there! 'Has Dupont been treating you well?'

'Very well,' replied Cathy, trying to settle herself in the chair and look relaxed. 'In fact, I was delighted that so much has been done so quickly.'

'Good. Otherwise, I would have had something to say to him,' he replied brusquely. 'So, have you anything to show me?'

'Oh, yes, I've been doing quite a lot of work in the library, looking up old maps and suchlike,' replied Cathy.

'And were they helpful?'

'Some of them.'

'Did you have much of a problem finding them? I'm afraid that my library sadly needs cataloguing, but good, private librarians are hard to find these days. Especially if they are only to be employed for a limited time.' His cold eyes held hers and she didn't flinch. But she had a horrid feeling that he knew something.

'As a student, I'm used to using libraries, Bernard. It took some doing but, in the end, I succeeded. Would you like to see my blueprint now?' He looked at his watch, then straight at her again. His lips curled at the corners.

'We could discuss them over lunch? Would

you like that?' It was the last thing she wanted; in fact, she felt like a moth wriggling under a pin. How she would manage to keep quiet, she didn't know, but her growing dislike of Bernard outweighed her moral dilemma. Also, if she said no, then he might get offended and what would happen to her project.

'That's very nice of you. But I'm afraid I'm not dressed for a restaurant. However . . .' she hesitated, hoping he would change his mind. Instead, he said,

'Why don't I run you down to Madame Laine's in the car? You can change, while I have a word with her.' There was no getting out of it.

'I was going to say,' replied Cathy, 'that I do have some other clothes with me. I could change here, if you don't mind waiting.' He was looking at her as if he was delighted by the idea.

'How enterprising of you,' he said. 'Of course.' He looked at his watch again. 'Shall we meet in, say, half-an-hour, or will it take longer?' The tiny hint of sarcasm did not escape her.

'Half-an-hour will be fine,' replied Cathy.

'I'll meet you on the terrace then. Half-an-hour. Excellent.' Cathy gathered up her things and with a slight smile, started to make for the door. 'Just a moment,' he said, raising his hand and picking up the phone. Cathy raised her eyebrows as he dialled a number and spoke.

87

'Charlotte? Will you come through and take Mam'selle Murdoch to a suitable bedroom. She wishes to change.'

Cathy had planned to go into one of the downstairs cloakrooms, that were palatial, but, several minutes later, she was following Charlotte silently up the grand staircase under the eyes of more Benoit ancestors, most of whom were a great deal handsomer than Bernard. In fact, one of them reminded her peculiarly of someone she was sure she'd met, but she couldn't think who. He had a steely, aristocratic expression.

The housekeeper left Cathy clutching her holdall in a very grand room, which also reminded her of several places where she'd stayed with her parents, when her father was in diplomatic service.

Cathy turned the key in the door and hurriedly took the dress, sprigged with delicate flowers, out of her holdall. It was somewhat crumpled, so she hung it from the golden handle of the tallboy and left her light sandals beneath.

Then she went into the bathroom, that was even grander. Unfortunately, being lined with mirrors, it revealed too clearly what a scruff she looked.

She had a very quick shower and managed not to wet her hair. When she emerged, wrapped in a luxurious white towel, she took a peek out of the window and saw Bernard pacing up and down the terrace below. A glance at her watch confirmed she still had fifteen minutes.

'He'll just have to wait, however manic he is,' she said, out loud, then grinned. Afterwards, she slipped on her dress and slicked on the minimum of make-up. Her sandals completed the whole.

Then Cathy sat down on the bed for a breather. Maybe she might find something out from Bernard about the mausoleum? She decided she could just bring it out in the conversation when she told him about the ha-ha. Then she thought about Luc again. She hoped Bernard wouldn't take her to the same restaurant Luc had. That would be truly awful! It would also make her very sad.

Two minutes before the half-hour was up, she was walking across the hall in the direction of the terrace.

It was then she had the creepy feeling she was being watched. She turned quickly and saw Charlotte hovering in a doorway. Their eyes met blankly, then the housekeeper disappeared into the room behind.

'Wonderful,' said Bernard, looking her up and down. 'You know, you look very much like your mother, as I remember her. Dear Rosalie.'

'Oh, dear,' quipped Cathy, as he ushered her to the car, an extremely large and sleek, dark blue BMW convertible with the top down. He opened the heavy door for her and she managed to get in gracefully. She wasn't too keen on the way he was looking at her legs. All of a sudden, Cathy knew that the next hour or two were going to be an ordeal she had to get through without letting anything slip.

Cathy could not have coped with lobster, but Bernard worked his way through it carefully, using a cut-glass finger bowl, brought by an attentive waiter. What else would he choose? thought Cathy, watching him picking over the carcass with white fingers.

'So far I approve of your plans, Cathy,' he said, discarding the lobster's last remains and wiping his fingers on the fine, linen serviette. 'By the way, do you like this restaurant? You haven't been here before, have you?'

'No, although Marie has pointed it out to me,' she lied, her stomach turning over. She was not a natural liar, but she was having to become one—and for what. Why was she lying for a man she hardly knew? Her fear about where they would eat had come true, and her spirits had taken a steep downturn, when Bernard had parked almost in the same place as Luc. They had been greeted by an inscrutable maitre d' on their arrival and been treated with the deference that such an important man as Bernard could command.

It had struck her later that Luc had been received in the same familiar, ingratiating way as Bernard. Probably it was such a good restaurant they attended to everyone similarly, but, surely, Luc was not of any local standing and he was only a student librarian. How could he afford to eat there? And run the Porsche?

Strangely, she hadn't thought of anything like that afterwards, because command suited him as it did Bernard. She had a horrible moment when she almost believed the respect Luc had earned was on account of his ill-gotten gains! A gentleman thief.

But, above all she wanted to trust him, although she had been on tenterhooks through the meal, in case one of the waiters made a chance remark about her earlier visit. Her anxiety about being discovered and questioned, coupled with her dislike of the way poor lobsters were treated, had made her settle for a vegetarian dish, which had turned out to be an excellent choice of aubergines and sauces. Yet it had made her feel slightly queasy.

'So far so good,' Bernard repeated. 'Now,' he added, settling back in his chair, 'what are your plans for the area bordering the pool? It's excellent for trout, although the fish do their best not to get caught. It needs someone who knows their haunts. Has Charlotte treated you to a fish breakfast yet?' Cathy took a moment to reply.

'Not yet,' she said quietly.

'It is worth fishing there, you know.'

'Is it? I don't.' She smiled, but her mouth

was quite dry. Did he suspect anything? She took a sip of wine. How could he? Then she recovered herself. 'I would like to build a ha-ha.' She wasn't sure if he would know what it is, but he did . . .' And later, to add a quiet place there with a seat.'

'So one may sit and think of friends, or even lovers.' She stiffened, but he didn't seem to notice her agitation as he was calling the waiter and asking for the dessert menu, which arrived directly.

'Yes, a place of meditation.' She hid her face behind it for a moment. 'Well, Cathy?'

She felt stronger now. 'I won't have a dessert, thank you.' She thought she might be sick if she did. 'I shall be working this afternoon.'

'And you do not have to worry about your figure.'

'I do,' she said, purposely waiving his compliment. She'd decided she was going to ask for what she wanted. She had to take some kind of control. 'I hope this isn't an insensitive question, but for whom was the mausoleum built?'

'It's a family tomb,' he said, 'My illustrious ancestors would never have dreamed being buried off their land. There are many generations of Benoits lying there. And, of course, in due time . . .' He paused ' . . . at the right time, I shall join them.'

'Oh, don't say that.' She had to say

something, out of politeness.

'My resting place has been prepared,' he added. 'You see, Cathy, I am somewhat like the Pharaoh. I like to know where I shall lie, when my time comes. It's very important when you bear an aristocratic name. Have you had a close look at the building?'

'I did walk round it,' she said. 'The angels are magnificent.'

'They were brought over from Italy around 1826 in the reign of Charles X,' he said. 'The king was known as a monarch, who wished to repair, rather than destroy, and my ancestors took their cue from him in the 19th century and re-built the mausoleum, exactly as it had been before, outside and in. Except, of course, for the angels.'

'Was it destroyed in the Revolution?' Cathy asked.

'Exactly! By ungrateful peasants. Our family had always looked after them. But they turned against us.'

For the first time, Bernard's face was flushed. Cathy had evidently hit a nerve.

'The mausoleum had stood there since the reign of Louis XIII in the 1600s, until a hundred and fifty years later, those peasants gave the tombs a good hammering and set it on fire.

'I suppose the angels were appointed as future guardians of our family. They certainly have a touch of the Gothic.' She didn't reply.

'Are you all right, Cathy? You look a little pale. Maybe this talk of tombs has upset you?'

'Of course not. I'm absolutely fine,' she said, leaning back. 'Will your men clear the undergrowth around the mausoleum? Otherwise, I can't do anything. I don't want to start planting, before all the earth is moved.'

'I have ordered them back on site. Strangely enough, Dupont thought that part should be left, but now he has his orders. Let's hope the ghosts of my noble ancestors do not mind the noise of excavators.'

'Thank you. That's very exciting,' she said, trying to look it. But all she could think of was that Luc would be entirely exposed and Bernard would be wandering around with a gun! She didn't know what was the matter with her, as that fact seemed the most important matter in the world.

'You're ready to get started, I can see,' said Bernard, that same cold smile on his face.

'I can't wait,' she said. 'How long do you think it will take to clear?'

'I've told them they must finish this afternoon, or I'll dock their wages.'

'I see. Good.' She smiled back, pretending to be in accord with his beastliness. You really are a mean person, Bernard, she thought.

'I'm glad you approve, although your mother was never entirely in agreement with some of my schemes.' The remark was so unexpected that Cathy was caught off guard.

94

'My mother?'

'So Marie hasn't told you?'

'Told me what?'

'That Rosalie and I were very much in love.'

'Good gracious.' Cathy tried to laugh it off. 'What a surprise!'

'She refused me, you know,' said Bernard calmly. 'I thought I wouldn't ever get over it. But I have—until now.'

'What do you mean?'

'I mean that now I have her very image in front of me again. You have brought it all back. We used to come here, you know . . .' Cathy didn't want to hear. 'You know . . . to eat, but then it was different. Just small tables, very intimate. Local fellows with bottles of wine. Bourgeoisie. But, in the end, she didn't want me . . .'

Cathy was hoping he'd stop. All she longed to do was get away. She didn't want to hear about her mother's amours. She remembered what Marie had said, He's had his chances. Was her mother one of those? Evidently.

'And Marie . . .' He was off again. ' . . . Marie was very fond of my brother . . . And he, her. We were an unwilling foursome.'

'You have a brother?' Cathy was so surprised.

'Did have, Cathy. He was younger than I. Unfortunately, we never got on. He was the youngest—charmant, and very spoiled by my parents . . . But the girls were inseparable,

95

naturellement. We went along with that. We two were unwilling always to be in each other's company. But I think he cared truly for Madame Laine, as I did Rosalie. As you English say, those were the days.'

'What happened?' Cathy dared to ask. She wanted to hear Marie's story too.

'What happens to us all. He died. Drowned. Near Biarritz. He is not in the mausoleum. They never found his body. The Atlantic wouldn't give it up.'

'I'm so sorry.' The explanation made Bernard seem less approachable, and more human.

'It was a long time ago. Now, I think we should go.' He consulted his watch. 'We both have work to do.' Minutes later, Bernard was paying for the bill with a gold card like Luc's . . .

Cathy didn't talk much on the way home, but let him instead. Finally, he told her that he had decided to act upon all she had done; that he was delighted with the scheme and would see it put into practice before she returned to England.

Then to her chagrin, he added, 'You should be proud of yourself being able to convince one of the most astute men in France to spend an inordinate amount of money on a wild patch. However,' he added, 'noble patronage has always flourished in France and I believe in keeping up with tradition.' Not only was he arrogant, but pompous as well!

She should have been ecstatic over the success of her very first project, but Cathy had other things to think about as the BMW slid along the lanes on its way back to the chateau. She had to find some way to warn Luc. She felt like a criminal herself, now that reason had deserted her. She only wanted to get back to her garden and work out her frustration, as well as plan what her next move was going to be.

CHAPTER EIGHT

What Bernard had said about his late brother was foremost in Cathy's mind as she finished as much as she could of another of Marie's lovely dinners.

In fact, besides her other and more dangerous plans for the evening, she had been thinking a lot about Marie loving the youngest Benoit. Otherwise, her afternoon had been filled by doing an enormous amount to further the project. She had ordered plants and soil and had even found Dupont and told him that Bernard approved entirely with all she'd planned and that his employer had agreed open-heartedly to go ahead with the project.

She had to admit she had felt a tiny satisfaction when the formerly uncooperative Frenchman had mildly agreed with everything she asked. Of course, his job would have been at risk if he had not. However, she felt inwardly that he blamed her for popping upon the scene and causing him and his team so much extra work.

She couldn't imagine how he was involved with Luc but she didn't trust him enough to let slip anything about her own involvement. No, she had to warn Luc herself. It did cross her mind that somehow, Dupont might let him know that, after his men had finished—which they would—there would be no cover for him. The mausoleum would be exposed totally and even the smallest glimmer of light could be seen from anyone watching at the chateau.

She was glad that the creative part of her brain still appeared to be working as she, herself, felt totally confused. Why did she want to risk even her life to help a man who she'd only met a few days ago? Yet, somewhere inside, she knew that, although she had promised herself, since Paul, that she wouldn't rely purely on her emotions again, she was doing just that with Luc. And that she would keep on doing it until she discovered the truth.

'Something serious must have happened with Bernard,' said Marie, folding her napkin. 'You've hardly said a word all evening.' She looked anxious.

'Oh, I'm sorry, Marie. Yes, something has happened but it isn't serious, it's good. Bernard has accepted everything and I can't help thinking about it all the time.' At least part of that was true.

'But that's wonderful! I'm very happy for you, dear,' replied Marie, getting up and coming round to give her a hug. Cathy felt awful. 'Did he take you out to lunch?'

'Yes, he did! I had to change at the chateau. I was covered in mud and . . .'

'Where did you go?' interposed Marie.

'He took me to the same place that Luc did.' Cathy could see alarm in Marie's eyes.

Cathy wanted to say, Don't worry, I won't harm him or you. I don't know what it's all about but I will tell you, I promise, when I've sorted it out for myself. Instead, she remained silent.

'You didn't mention . . .'

'No, I didn't mention Luc. It was a bit difficult but I remembered what you said.'

'Thank you. Of course, it isn't that important, but Luc is a nice young man and I wouldn't like to think that either of us was responsible for him losing his job. It's a pity you didn't get on though. You would have made a sweet couple.'

'I didn't say we didn't get on, just that I was thinking more carefully about how I felt before I jumped in feet first.' Cathy smiled. At least that was a lie. Suddenly, she wondered if Luc had discussed how he felt about her to Marie. She really wanted to find out but it was impossible, seeing as she wasn't supposed to have seen him with her friend!

'I'm proud of you, Cathy,' said Marie suddenly.

'Why?' Praise was the least thing that Cathy expected.

'That you've been able to shake off the problems you had when you came here. But I thought it would do you good, being with me again at this house. You've brought . . .' Marie hesitated. 'I know it sounds silly but you've brought life to the old place again.'

100

'Thank you, Marie, I don't deserve it. Anyway, you have lots of friends.' Cathy felt extremely guilty.

'But I still miss my best friend and, now you're here, it's like having Rosalie back again.' That's what Bernard had said. Cathy knew she looked like her mother but was she really anything like her at all. Before she could stop herself, the question slipped out. 'Marie, did Mother have any special boyfriend when you were young?'

'Why do you ask?'

'It was something Bernard said.'

'Did he?' Marie's wise eyes regarded her from the other side of the table. 'Then you probably know the answer to that.' Cathy flushed. 'I suppose he told you that he was in love with your mother?'

'It's just that I remember you saying he'd had plenty of chances.'

'Well, he was the most eligible bachelor for miles around. Quite a playboy in his youth.' Cathy couldn't imagine the stiff and severe middle-aged man being anything else but what he was. 'He held a torch for her. It was because she wouldn't give in. He wanted the only thing he couldn't have and he didn't get it.'

'So, it wasn't love, just acquisition.' Cathy had suspected something like that. She couldn't imagine her mother choosing to be with Bernard.

101

'I wouldn't say that. I think he loved her in his own way but she knew what kind of life she'd have had if she'd married him. And her refusal made him very bitter. But, in the beginning, we all had some good times together.' Marie had a faraway look in her eyes. Cathy sat, trying to decide if she dare ask about Bernard's brother but it would be insensitive and tactless. Marie caught her glance. 'Did he also tell you about Paul?'

'Paul?'

'His brother?'

'Briefly.' Cathy wished she hadn't pried, given the look on Marie's face. It had a growing softness about it as if she was transported to another place. And Cathy realised that she did want to hear after all that true love still existed, whatever had been her own experience of the opposite. She wanted to feel that there was still hope.

'Paul, as I think you know, was Bernard's younger brother. As he was never likely to inherit, like many younger sons, he did not have the burden of the estate on his shoulders. But he would have suited the role. He was a very different man from his elder brother.'

She smiled. 'He was serious and caring, while Bernard revelled in his own good fortune. He felt that, if Bernard went on like he did, frittering away the estate's resources, planning one scheme for it and then another, his heritage and our village that depended

102

upon it, would invariably be ruined.

'Of course, the war had taken its toll and the house had been raided by the Nazis anyway. Many priceless artefacts had disappeared so Paul decided that he was going to try and recover them and he actually succeeded in having several of them returned. Paul was a countryman at heart, whereas Bernard was very much like those ancestors of his who had perished in the Revolution, dissolute, arrogant and out for his own ends.'

Marie sighed. 'The place would have been very different if Paul had lived. But . . .' She shrugged expressively as only the French can do. 'Bernard and he quarrelled violently and he left permanently. He was on a business trip to Cannes with his wife when . . .'

'His wife?' Cathy was shocked. 'But I thought that . . .'

'You thought that he loved me?'

'I'm sorry, but . . . yes?'

'Bernard told you that, of course.' Cathy nodded.

'I did, but I have a name for being wise, my dear.'

'I don't understand,' said Cathy. Marie leaned over and patted her hand.

'I wanted him a great deal . . . To marry him . . . It was an extremely difficult decision.' She sighed deeply.

'Please don't upset yourself, Marie. I wish I hadn't said anything now.'

'No, the truth is better, dear. I've learned that. I loved Paul, madly and crazily, but I had a secret.' She bit her lip and, to Cathy's horror, tears filled her eyes.

'Please don't, Marie,' cried Cathy.

'It has tortured me for many years. Of course, your mother knew.' Cathy couldn't bear to think what was coming. 'I . . . No, my father died of a horrible disease, a genetic condition. My mother and I were forced to watch his slow demise and I vowed that I would never marry or have children in case I passed it on to my own.

'In those days there was no genetic screening as there is now to find out if I was a carrier. It was take your chances. But I couldn't take that chance to have a son—and that was what Paul wanted, of course. Children.' Marie had an expression on her face that almost broke Cathy's heart. 'No son of mine would be born into this world to suffer what my father did. So I refused him and I am happy to say that, finally, he found some happiness too . . .'

'Please, Marie, don't tell me any more. I feel terrible at having asked.' Cathy leaped out of her chair and came and put her arms round Marie and laid her cheek against hers. 'Don't cry, please.'

'I'm not crying, Cathy. I have been happy with my memories. And you have been like my own daughter every time you come here. I have your mother to thank for that.' Marie took out her handkerchief and wiped her eyes. 'So that's my little story. You can see why I want you to be happy, Cathy, to find someone you really love.'

'I want to, Marie,' replied Cathy desperately. She was almost in tears too.

'And you will, I promise you. Just wait a bit longer. But be brave enough to follow your heart. Don't let anything put you off. It's always best to tell—and know—the truth. I don't regret what I did, but although I paid the price, my heart has been with Paul Benoit all my life.'

Marie got up, then threw back her shoulders as if some great weight had been lifted. 'Come on, let's clear the table.' Marie picked up the two plates and looked across at Cathy. 'Anyway, what are your plans for tonight? You can't be working all the time.'

Should Cathy tell Marie everything right now? She just didn't know. But her friend had told her to follow her heart.

'Nothing very exciting.' Cathy looked Marie in the eyes and, suddenly, she was sure the older woman had an idea what she was planning. Cathy was also confident that whatever was happening at the chateau, it could not be that bad. Marie was too good to let anyone down or to be involved with anything shady. 'I think I'd like to go for a ride,' she added meaningfully.

'Good. It's a beautiful night. But please be careful.'

'Of course I will.'

'Take your phone.'

'I never go anywhere without it. It's such a lovely night that . . .' she hesitated, whether to reveal a little more, ' . . . that I may be late.'

Once again, Marie didn't try to stop her or even to warn her.

She only said calmly, 'I'd like to come . . . but I'm very tired. All that emotion, I suppose.' They smiled at each other and again Cathy felt that Marie understood what she had to do and that she would back her up if need be.

An hour later, Cathy turned round at the brow of the ill and looked back at Chinon. The floodlights had already been turned on the castle and below in the village, several lights flickered in the night wind.

Cathy had kept close to the verge. She hadn't taken her bike as she'd told Marie. She wasn't going to leave it where it might be stolen. If this had been an ordinary summer evening and she had not been so preoccupied with her own thoughts, she would have lingered in the dusk to smell the night scents. It was a lovely walk up to the chateau but her head was full of the plan she'd made. She certainly wasn't going in the front way!

She would make for the mausoleum, entering the estate by one of the back gates.

106

This meant leaving the road and climbing over a few fences and stiles, one of which she was considering now. Luckily, the French landscape in that area was not a patchwork of fields. The terrain was open, broken now and again by a few small woods and spinneys.

The path she had chosen led through one of the latter and on to Bernard's land. She had to negotiate an electric fence which had been put up to keep the deer in, but she was adept at jumping over those anyway.

Her hair was tied back and she was dressed suitably; black jeans, a short-sleeved T-shirt under her black hooded sweatshirt and her boots. She was carrying the map and a small torch. Once again she checked her phone which was vital. She hoped she would get a signal if she needed it as the pool was surrounded by trees, but she wasn't going to worry about that now.

The thing that worried her most was the idea that Bernard might be on the prowl! She was sure that he suspected something was going on. She'd decided that, if the worst came to the worst, she'd shout out who she was and he certainly wouldn't shoot her on sight.

It was a horrible thought that came back sharply as she jumped over the electric fence. She'd never done anything illegal before now. Then she consoled herself with the fact that she was an employee of Bernard's, at least for the summer, so if anyone else challenged her over the fields, she would be able to explain she was on the payroll. But all these worries of hers were probably unfounded.

Whatever happened, she was determined to go to the mausoleum and find Luc. If he wasn't there, if he didn't come, she'd have to think again, but she was willing to wait; for how long she wasn't sure but, somewhere inside, she felt that he would be there and she intended to make him explain. Funnily enough, she had no fear of his reaction at all.

As she climbed over the next stile, she replaced all her anxieties with determination, although at one point she found that her hands were trembling . . .

Everything went well from then on. Skirting the pool was a little tricky owing to the marshy ground and thicket but she kept well away from the edge. The moon was rising which threw a little light but thankfully, not too much.

Her first glance of the mausoleum, its white surface reflecting the light, made her shiver again and she had to stop and take a breath. Was she really brave enough to approach it and see if anyone was inside? She thought of all those dead Benoits lying there, guarded by their angels. If Luc was inside, would he have closed the door behind him? Then she wouldn't be able to get in. At that moment, she wished she hadn't come but a moment later she started, sure she'd seen a tiny glimmer of light coming from the entrance.

He's there, she said to herself, or someone is. Pulling up her hood, she found herself breathing a silent prayer as she approached as quietly as she could. Every step she took, she fancied she could hear her feet squelching in the mud.

Perhaps she should go home right now? It wasn't her business. But Cathy had never been a quitter. A moment later, she had slipped inside the entrance, under the angels' watchful eyes. They looked extremely frightening at night, like something out of a horror movie.

The light was coming from the door. The mausoleum was open. Breathing deeply, Cathy pushed at the heavy wood and squeezed inside. She found herself standing at the head of a deep flight of stairs. The place smelled of age and damp, almost suffocating her and down there she could hear tapping. She was sure it was the sound of a hammer. Luc must be a grave robber as well.

Biting her lip, she descended carefully, making sure she didn't slip. She was so glad her boots had no metal studs. As it was, their heavy soles rendered them noiseless. Another door was ajar at the bottom.

She peeped through. She could see now why there was only a glimmer of light; the heavy industrial torch was standing in a corner, draped with sacking which made the chamber dim. It was swivelled in the direction of the loud hammering which had only seemed like a faint tapping above. But she couldn't see at what, from that angle.

Her eyes were drawn to a part of the wall that was revealed by the light. She closed them momentarily. A recess revealed a skull and bones! She opened the door a crack farther and craned her neck, oblivious to everything except trying to see who was in there. She didn't notice the hammering had stopped!

In that one moment of inattention, the scream stuck in her throat as her arm was jerked forward roughly and she fell forwards, face down, on to the floor. A minute later, a hand dragged back her hood. A moment of silence ensued. Then she felt the hand on her shoulder. It was gentle this time. 'Are you OK?' She knew the voice. Tears of relief filled her eyes. 'Have I hurt you?'

'I . . .' She could hardly speak. Everything hurt. Her nose felt strange. Then she rolled over. There was utter shock on his face. Luc was dressed all in black, kneeling beside her.

He helped her sit up. She was holding her arm and, for the first time, was conscious that blood was dripping from her nose. Had she broken it? She tried to wipe it with her hand. He handed her a cloth.

'Ow!' She grimaced as she touched her nose.

'For God's sake, Cathy, what do you think you're doing here?'

110

'I could ask you the same thing!' she replied bravely, holding the cloth to her face. It smelled of oil. 'Here!' She handed it back to him and began to ferret in her pocket with her good hand. Finally, she brought out a clean handkerchief. Then she noticed the big chisel lying beside her. His eyes followed hers.

'I could have hit you with that.'

'It's a good thing you didn't,' she said, 'but you nearly pulled my arm out of joint. And I think you've broken my nose.'

'I don't think so,' he said, examining it carefully. 'You just banged it when you fell. I'm sorry,' he said, sitting back on his heels. 'You know you shouldn't be here.'

'I'm here because I knew you'd be,' she said, rubbing her arm. She felt terrible—but it was her own fault. At least, he'd caught her. It could have been Bernard.

'How?' He frowned.

'I heard you and Dupont talking.'

'You did what? You were listening to our conversation?'

She nodded defiantly. 'I saw you in Bernard's study. Trying to break open his desk and crack open the safe.' By the look on his face now, she knew he wouldn't hurt her but she could see the frustration. 'Are you a crook?' He began to rub her arm as well. She pulled herself away. 'I want the truth.'

'Why?'

'Because I . . . I have to know.'

111

'Is that all?'

'It's enough.'

'I don't think it is, Cathy. I can't explain what I was doing.' He looked round. 'Nor what I am doing here. I want you to go—now. And forget that you've seen me. I should never have asked you out. I don't want you to be involved in any of this.'

'But I am involved. I'm here, aren't I? I saw you in the house and do you know what? I almost called the police. And then, when Bernard came back ...'

'You didn't tell him?'

'No, I didn't. I was going to but Marie asked me not to.'

'Does she know you're here?' Cathy shook her head.

'No-one does. I came because ... because I care about you. I didn't want to believe that you're a criminal. And now here you are— breaking open a tomb! What are you doing, Luc? Who are you?'

'I'm not going to answer your questions. Go home, Cathy, and forget you've seen me.'

'That won't be easy. Are you going to forget all about me?' It was his turn to shake his head. 'Then trust me, please.'

'I daren't. If Bernard knows you are involved in this, God knows what he'll do.'

'He'll do the same to you.'

'No, he won't,' said Luc vehemently.

'Why?'

'Because . . .' Cathy could see he was trying to find the right thing to say, ' . . . because it will be more difficult. I am . . .'

'Who are you, Luc?'

He put a hand to his forehead and rubbed it. 'If I tell you who I am, it won't make a difference. Why are you doing this, Cathy?'

'Because I like you,' said Cathy, getting to her feet. 'I can't bear to see you stealing and robbing tombs.'

Luc shook his head desperately. 'You're better than this. Or . . . is this the way you make your money? Answer me, please.'

He was staring at her, biting his lip.

'If I tell you the truth, will you go away?'

'I don't know,' said Cathy. He gestured helplessly.

'So you're going to stay here until I'm picked up by the police or Bernard finds us and blows both our heads off?' His brutality frightened her, but she persisted.

'He wouldn't do that!'

'Oh, yes, he would. You don't know him like I do. He's . . .'

'Manic?' He walked away from her, back towards the tomb, chisel in hand. 'Marie said he was. She spoke highly of you, though. Does she know what you're doing here?'

'Yes, Marie knows! You're very hard to get rid of, Cathy.'

'So I've been told,' she replied, standing her ground. She watched as he picked up the

113

chisel and approached her.

'If I tell you that Bernard and I have an old score to settle, would that satisfy you?'

'No,' she said.

'Look, this isn't a game. I have no time. I came here to do a job and I'm going to do it.'

'Are you going to hit me with that?' she asked lightly, although she felt very scared. Suddenly, he caught her by the shoulders. 'Ow!'

'Sorry. Don't be stupid. All right, listen. This old score means a great deal to a lot of people. To Marie, to Dupont, Charlotte, the lot of them, the whole village.'

'And you're saving them?'

'I'm trying, but I never will unless I can prise the blasted lid off this tomb,' he said, retreating and picking up the hammer.

'Can I help?'

'Yes, by going home and keeping quiet. Now will you let me get on with what I'm doing.' He sighed. 'You could watch the door if you intend to stay. But don't blame me for what happens to you.' With that, he turned on his heel and began attacking the lid again.

She watched as if in a dream. It was so unreal. She looked round at the skulls and bones lying on shelves, the shadowy marble and stone tombs. It was a charnel house as well as a resting place for Bernard's ancestors.

'What are you looking for?' she ventured. He didn't answer so she stood by the door,

114

feeling bruised all over mentally and physically. It was her own fault. She'd found him and was none the wiser. He said he was doing everyone a favour. How could he be? Should she run now? But her feet wouldn't move. It was as if invisible shackles were holding her.

'Aah!' He groaned. The chisel had worked and the great lid moved.

'I'll help!' she cried and a moment later she was at his side. Together they strained and pushed until, with an enormous grating sound, the lid fell back. She didn't dare look but she heard him swear.

'Another coffin.' A moment later he had heaved himself up and disappeared inside the tomb. 'Hand me the chisel and the hammer.' His hand appeared and she placed them in his open palm. You've done it now, Cathy, she said to herself. She could hear desperate smashing and grinding inside which seemed to go on for ages. Then silence.

'What's happened?' she asked, still not daring to peep over the edge. But he didn't reply. Is he hurt? she thought. Then to her utter relief he climbed out, holding a small casket shaped like a house. He sat down on the floor.

'Give me that,' he ordered, indicating a pointed tool lying by a heavy rucksack. She obeyed. With wide eyes, she watched him open the casket with one blow.

115

He sat, staring. 'Grace a Dieu. It's here!' he said. Then, he put a dirty hand up to his eyes and wiped away what were, unmistakably, tears. The sophisticated young man, who lived in a tower and drove a Porsche, was crying before her very eyes. 'It's here! I was right after all.' She dropped on her knees beside him, every instinct telling her to comfort him.

'Look, Cathy.' He put in his hand carefully and withdrew his prize. Cathy gasped. It wasn't gold or jewels as she'd suspected, but a roll of vellum, still sealed at the edge.

'What is it?' she whispered.

'It's what I've been looking for. For the whole of last year after I . . .' He stopped and drew in a deep breath as if to stop himself saying too much. 'I knew I was right.' His mood had changed to one of triumph. Then to her astonishment, he jumped up, pulled her into his arms and began to dance around. Next moment, he kissed her hard. 'Now what's Bernard going to do, my Cathy?' he said triumphantly . . .

'This,' said a voice and both of them swung round to face the muzzle of a double-barrelled shotgun. Cathy screamed as Luc pulled her to him.

'You won't get away with it, Bernard,' he said in a voice as hard as Bernard's.

'Won't I? This time you have gone too far, my dear nephew,' snarled Bernard, coming out of the shadows into the light. He stared at

Cathy. 'So, mam'selle, you throw my hospitality back in my face?' Cathy couldn't speak. His nephew! Why hadn't she guessed? Luc was Paul's son!

'Let her go, Bernard. Your quarrel is with me, not Cathy,' he said.

'Just like the past. Ganging up on me. You're more like your mother than I thought you were, my dear.'

'I can see why she didn't love you,' burst out Cathy, able to speak at last.

'Quiet, Cathy,' hissed Luc.

'So Marie has told you about us, has she?' snarled Bernard. 'Did she tell you that if it wasn't for this boy here, I would have been able to do what I like with my inheritance, without anyone's interference. But he's still not satisfied, even though he's my heir and will inherit my money. Instead, he goes about stealing from me.'

'You shouldn't have hidden the evidence, Bernard,' Luc said, facing up to him. 'You knew I'd find the document in the end. I'd have gone on looking for it until I stopped you doing what you intend to.

'Do you know why he went to New York, Cathy?' Luc added. 'He's ready to sell the chateau to an American firm of developers, who'll do God knows what with it. And I intend to stop him. Do you know what this is, Cathy?' He pointed to the parchment. 'Shall I tell her, Bernard?'

117

'What you tell her now is immaterial.' He shrugged. 'No-one else will ever read it.' Cathy felt herself go cold. Was Bernard going to carry out his threat? Had Luc been right when he said that if Bernard found out he'd blow both their heads off. Right now, the argument seemed horribly plausible! She felt fear run right through her body, making her legs shake.

'Marie began this . . .' said Luc.

'Marie?' asked Cathy.

'Yes. A year ago, she contacted me, having got wind of Bernard's plans. I had never been welcome in the house where my father grew up. I remind my uncle too much of him.'

He threw a hostile glance in Bernard's direction. 'He never had any time for his brother. And, even then, he was hatching his plans; doing up the chateau so it would be more saleable. It was then that Marie told me my father had once related to her the existence of an old law regarding the chateau.

'My mediaeval ancestor, whose bones are now nothing but dust, who lay in there quietly until tonight,' he pointed to the open tomb, 'had set down on his will that the chateau and the estate were only to be used and held for the heirs' personal use in perpetuity. In other words, no unscrupulous descendant could sell them off for his own profit.

'According to my father, a legend also existed telling of a copy of the document being kept in the library, whereas the original was

118

interred in the tomb of his ancestor. What Bernard did not know was that my father had told Marie and that she'd told me. In fact, he invited me to the chateau about two years ago. I realised then it was to try and discover if I knew anything about the document. Of course, at that stage, I did not.

'But after Marie's news, I determined to find it; first the copy, to verify what it said and, after, the original. But I had no idea where in the library the copy was hidden, until I followed the clues; only to find the document gone. I realised only in the last couple of weeks that Bernard had disposed of it or hidden it, but I had to try his desk and the safe and any other place it might be.'

Bernard was smiling, the same, creepy smile that didn't reach his eyes. 'And, mam'selle, once I discovered that young Luc here was using my property as if it was his own, turning up whenever I was away, I was determined to catch him.'

'How did you find out?' asked Cathy, her eyes fixed on the shotgun.

'One day I decided to visit the tower on spec. It was the most likely place to find you, given that my brother had his rooms up there. His no-go area!' Bernard turned to Luc. 'You or the housekeeper had been careless. I discovered the most inoffensive of things, a biro. Imagine! Not something marked with the Benoit crest, but a common biro, with the

History Department, Sorbonne stamped upon it. It had fallen somehow into the folds of one of the bed curtains. I put two and two together. Who had studied History at the Sorbonne, but my precious nephew?

'After that, I engaged a private detective, who informed me of your frequent visits in my absence. You betrayed yourself, Luc, but I promise you, that the rest of my staff will pay for their disloyalty by losing their livelihoods.'

'You're a disgrace to our name,' retorted Luc in a cold voice.

'So I've been told by a variety of my enemies,' he responded. 'As for you, mam'selle, I am aware that you were invited by my nephew to his ivory tower. I do not think you will see your pet project come to fruition.'

'Let her go, Bernard. She knew nothing.'

'It looks like it. Remember, I caught you kissing. Cathy is in it up to the neck as the English say. It's a pity that I shall never get that garden finished.'

'What do you intend to do with us?' Luc asked. Then Cathy felt his hand slip into hers.

'No funny business! Get away from her.' They parted quickly. 'I think that I shall either shoot you here and have the tomb re-sealed . . . Or . . .' Cathy felt sick. ' . . . Or I shall take you out on to the estate. It would be a natural mistake to shoot a couple of poachers.'

'You'll be found out, Bernard,' said Luc flatly. 'You'll be a murderer. Besides, Dupont knows I'm here.'

'Dupont will be paid well and promoted.'

'He's loyal.'

'Where money is concerned, no-one is loyal. They will all keep their mouths shut.'

'You're mad,' said Luc, but Cathy felt the alarm in his voice. 'Kill me, but let her go.'

'How touching,' said Bernard. 'I am coming round to the idea of killing you outside at the moment but, first hand over the parchment.' He indicated with the gun and, unwillingly, Luc picked it up. Cathy could see that there was nothing either of them could do. Ideas were racing through her head. Once they were outside, they could run into the trees, but then they would be shot in the back . . . It was too horrible to think of . . .

Bernard lifted the gun and Cathy began to shake again. It was her own fault but, somehow, she believed that this could not be the end. It was ludicrous. She was on her holidays!

'Now, move,' Bernard was approaching. 'The parchment. Throw it over here!' Luc stood still. He didn't move at all. Suddenly, she wanted him to beg, but she could see, by his expression, that it was the last thing he would do. His ancestors probably looked like that going to the guillotine. 'Do what I say!' Bernard threatened. 'Move!' he repeated.

'No, don't! Stay where you are!'

Bernard swung round.

'Thank God!' said Luc, 'I thought you'd never come.'

'Marie!' cried Cathy. The Frenchwoman put up her hand, warning her to stay still. She, too, was dressed in black, her hair, swept up, but still elegant. And she had no gun. She'll be at his mercy too, thought Cathy. Bernard was smiling.

'Put that down, Bernard,' she said, 'you're not going to murder anyone.' His eyes were narrow and his throat was working as if he was about to speak. He lifted the gun and backing, directed it at Marie as well. 'Put it down,' she repeated, 'you can't win. Armed police are waiting outside.'

'I don't care. We'll all die together, you, the youngsters and then I'll turn it on myself.'

'Don't be stupid, Bernard, this has all got out of hand,' she replied calmly, as if speaking to a child. 'You were always hot-headed, threatening things you didn't carry out.'

She's so brave, thought Cathy. She looked down at her hands, which were sweating. Perspiration was rolling off her forehead, although she felt very cold. At that moment, Luc took her hand again and Bernard jerked the gun. Marie continued.

'You can't kill them, Bernard, they're only young. You and I have had our lives. But look at them, they are in love. You remember what it was like to be in love with Rosalie? How I loved Paul? Look at them. Will you destroy something else you love? Listen to me, Bernard, before it's too late. If you kill them and me, and afterwards yourself, what good will it have done? You're not a bad man, Bernard. I know that, otherwise I wouldn't still be friends with you.

'I've forgiven you for what you did to Paul. Why can't you make it up with his son? Luc is like him and, now, you have a second chance. He'll help you to make the chateau everything you want.'

'He doesn't want to see it sold. Why do you want to sell it? Tell me, Bernard, why? Wasn't it enough that the Nazis plundered it? Paul did everything he could to restore it and you've done a good job since. Don't let that all go to waste. Let's work together.

'Besides, remember the police. I had a very difficult job to persuade them to let me come in on my own. Don't let my efforts go to waste. This can be sorted out. You can say you thought that the tomb was being robbed; that you came in and found it was your nephew . . .'

'Be quiet,' Bernard said. 'Don't you ever stop talking? Luc is trying to destroy me.'

'Can't you see he's not? I always thought you were astute. You've got this all out of proportion. Now put the gun down.'

'He hates me, like Paul did,' said Bernard. 'We can never work this out.' Marie turned to Luc.

'Luc . . . Luc!' Cathy could see that Marie's

eyes were begging him to reinforce her words. She looked up at his set face. He was as stubborn as Bernard! Brave, but stubborn. She had to do something herself.

'Luc, please, I don't want to die,' cried Cathy. 'I've only just found you. I love you!' He stared at her. 'Please tell him that you don't hate him. That you forgive him. Please!'

He looked down into her face, then across at his uncle, who was aiming at them. Then his expression changed.

'What Marie says is true. I forgive you for what you did to my father, not because I'm afraid of you, but I love this girl—and I don't want us to die.' He put his arm round her shoulders and drew her to him. Cathy began to sob, as she clung close. Would Bernard listen to anything? Her eyes were closed as Marie spoke again.

'You see, anything can be worked out, Bernard. They're coming down.' Cathy opened her eyes to see Bernard lower his gun. A second later, the door crashed wide to reveal, first of all, two policemen in full body armour, with guns pointing, followed by two more.

'Drop the gun! Get over there,' one shouted. Bernard obeyed.

'You, out!' They indicated Cathy, Luc and Marie towards the door and up the steps . . . Cathy thought she was going to faint, as the night air hit her in the face.

A moment later, Luc was holding her up,

124

because her legs buckled and she fainted . . . When she came to, as if in a dream, with Luc bending over her, fanning her, she could hear Marie saying, 'It's all right, inspector, it was as I thought. When Monsieur Benoit discovered his nephew and his girlfriend inside the mausoleum, I'm afraid, he became rather angry. He's been under a lot of stress lately. I'm very sorry that I had to call you out, but I'm an old friend of the family, as you know. I'll request Bernard's solicitor to meet him at the station.'

The inspector looked extremely severe. 'We've had some problems with Monsieur Benoit and poachers before, Madame Laine, but this has to stop. I didn't know that Monsieur had a nephew.'

'Of course, you didn't, inspector. There's been family friction between them for a long time, but I think that, after this, it might be sorted out, once and for all.'

'It better be,' replied the inspector grimly. 'I'm afraid you are all going to have to give a statement, especially you two,' he added, indicating Luc and Cathy. 'What the hell do you think you were doing breaking into a tomb anyway? We have laws against that kind of thing in France.'

'I'll be happy to face the consequences of my actions,' replied Luc clearly, 'but no blame is attached to this young lady. She only came to find me. I'm afraid I'd forgotten we had a date.'

'Well, she'll still have to make a statement,' snapped the inspector. 'Are you feeling all right now, mam'selle?' At that moment, the police squad emerged, escorting Bernard, whose face was set, like a white mask, in the moonlight. Seconds later, he was being pushed into a police Jeep, which bumped away over the flat, cleared ground of Cathy's garden.

Very soon after, Cathy and Marie watched as Luc was taken away in another vehicle, still clutching the roll of vellum.

It was their turn next. They got into the inspector's car. 'I've never been arrested before,' said Cathy in a small voice. She still felt sick. 'You were so brave, Marie. You saved our life. What do you think will happen to them?'

'I don't know, but whatever does, they both have good lawyers. They certainly won't go to prison. And I promise you, Luc will be back to you in no time. That's when we'll find out if the Benoits are still as stubborn a lot as they ever were but, somehow, I think that you and I are going to be able to persuade them to be less aristocratic,' smiled Marie. 'Now, stop worrying.'

CHAPTER NINE

The chateau had never looked so beautiful as it did that late summer's day. Nature had poured all her energy into making every flower burst into profusion of perfume, and the roses most of all.

At the edge of the white rose beds, scarlet geraniums spilled on to the paths, that were not bordered by the box; and at the edge of the red rose gardens was a carpet of white.

Cathy sat with Luc in the shade at the end of the parterre. 'Yes, I think one of these would be very nice overlooking the ha-ha,' she said, stroking the smooth wood of the rustic seat. She was hoping to get her garden finished soon, but she had so many other things to do. 'Don't the roses smell wonderful? Sometimes, I think they're my favourite flowers and, then, I change my mind as I look at all the others.'

'I hope you haven't done so about me,' he said gently.

'What?' She opened them.

'Changed your mind?'

'How could I?' she asked. 'After all we've been through.'

'I didn't think Bernard would shoot,' he replied sombrely, 'but it wasn't a moment I'd care to repeat.'

'I did. At one point I thought we'd had it.

When you stood there with that look on your face!' She grimaced.

'What look?' He feigned innocence.

'You know. The expression that your noble ancestor on the grand staircase is wearing. That steely, aristocratic look, which says, "Do your worst, but don't mess with me!"'

'Oh, him,' smiled Luc. 'In fact, he did come to a bad end.' He made a quick stroke across his neck, then smiled at Cathy's expression. 'I shouldn't joke about such things, should I?'

'No. At least, you and Bernard are talking to each other. You've made it up, haven't you?' She still felt a little worried, although the two of them had seen sense. Marie said that it would take a very long time for them to see eye to eye after so many years of hostility.

'I don't know about that,' replied Luc maddeningly. 'He's a selfish, old beast. But, anyway, he's sunning himself in Monaco at the moment, keeping his head down and licking his wounds regarding the fine. He was lucky to get off with only that. After all, he once did actually shoot a poacher.'

'Thank goodness you got off too. To be fair, we can't expect Bernard to take on board what the parchment said, without some problems,' said Cathy. 'Anyway, I don't care about Bernard, but I want us to be happy; and that means inviting him to the wedding.'

'Over my dead body.'

'It might have been,' reminded Cathy. 'At

least, he's promised not to sell the estate and taken you on as . . .' She was struggling for the French expression. 'Oh, I don't know what he called it.' She grimaced at Luc, who lifted his eyebrows.

'Never mind what he called it. What he actually meant was, "you can look after the place, while I'm away, enjoying myself."'

'But that's what you wanted, wasn't it?'

'Yes.' His arm tightened around her. She winced. 'Oh, sorry, did I hurt you?' He kissed her shoulder.

'Not really, it's still a bit sore though.' She'd had to have a course of physiotherapy. 'Anyway, being lord of the manor is a much better job than being a fake librarian!'

'I agree,' he said. 'But why are we talking about the past? Let's talk about us.' He cradled her in both arms now, something that she loved. She snuggled up to him. 'Now we've set a date, I'm satisfied. I thought you were going to give me the boot when you took so long to decide on an answer to my proposal.'

'I was being careful—for once,' said Cathy. 'After all, getting married to a French aristocrat is a life-changing decision. I really wanted to be a gardener.' She laughed at his expression.

'You're a tease,' he said, kissing her until she was breathless. When he stopped, he added, 'You can still be in charge of the gardens.'

'What? The whole lot?' She looked so shocked that he laughed.

'Whatever you want. You can plant roses, lilies, carnations, everything, even dig your ha-ha yourself, while I go fishing.'

'You can't. You'll have too much to do.'

'Just you wait,' he replied. 'I shall be down at that pool every day and bring fish home for my bride for breakfast.'

'No thank you,' she said indignantly. 'It's cruel. And how you can hit them on the head, I just don't know.'

'Shall I let you into a little secret,' he asked.

'Not another!' she joked.

'The day you and I met, when I was fishing . . . I didn't kill them.'

'I heard you,' protested Cathy.

'No, they were thrashing about, when I threw them back in. You had your eyes closed.'

'What about the stick and the knapsack?' she accused.

'I had my burglar's tools in there. I'd been trying to jemmy the door. I had to tell you something. I had been fishing, but I promise you, I didn't kill them. I'm not as bloodthirsty as Uncle Bernard.' She laughed out loud again at the twinkle in those mischievous, dark-brown eyes.

'So you promise we won't have fish for breakfast,' she joked.

'Only haddock, when your English friends come to stay. Anyway, how did you come to be

130

stuck in the brambles?' he teased.

'I wasn't stuck.' Cathy's eyes flashed. 'I was negotiating them.'

'Ma cherie,' he said softly, his voice changing, 'do you know when I fell in love with you first?' She shook her head; it was difficult to reply as he was covering her neck with tiny kisses and she was reeling from his touch.

'When I looked into your eyes and picked that enormous bramble out of your pretty hair.' The smile she had grown to love curled up his mouth. She wasn't going to disagree. Instead, she murmured in acquiescence but, as they went on playing the games that only lovers can play, she was thinking about her dream again.

Her knight was as handsome and brave as she'd ever imagined, even though he had plucked her out of a bramble bush, rather than saving her from a dragon! And now he was hers for keeps.

Wasn't that what any damsel had ever wanted?